I0749212

Materials for All Future Historians

by

Tito Perdue

Books by Tito Perdue

Lee (1991)
The New Austerities (1994)
Opportunities in Alabama Agriculture (1994)
The Sweet-Scented Manuscript (2004)
Fields of Asphodel (2007)
The Node (2011)
Morning Crafts (2013)
Reuben (2014)
The Builder: William's House I (2016)
The Churl: William's House II (2016)
The Engineer: William's House III (2016)
The Bachelor: William's House IV (2016)
Cynosura (2017)
Philip (2017)
Though We Be Dead, Yet Our Day Will Come (2018)
The Bent Pyramid (2018)
The Philatelist (2018)
The Smut Book (2018)
The Gizmo (2019)
Love Song of the Australopiths (2020)

Materials for All Future Historians

by

Tito Perdue

Standard American Publishing Company-
Brent, Alabama
2020

Cover image: Details from
Albrecht Dürer, *Saint Jerome in His Study*, 1514

Cover design by Kevin Slaughter

Hardcover ISBN: 978-1-64264-162-2
Paperback ISBN: 978-1-64264-163-9
E-book ISBN: 978-1-64264-164-6

Contents

One

He was a bleak sort of person, and his home, such as it was, sat atop a hill in a rural district of his native state. Other than that, you should know that his late beloved wife, ensconced forever in a vacuum-packed block of transparent plastic, slept next to him on the elevated bed.

He possessed perhaps some three or four thousand books arranged according to color and size, an impractical system that made it difficult for him to retrieve what he wanted at any particular time. He might for example be in search of volume two of the Rosenthal version of al-Tabari, only to end up starting at the beginning and going through the full collection before he hit upon what he wanted. And even then he was likely as not to be distracted by some other title before he got there.

He was a fastidious man certainly—he admitted that—and wanted his surroundings to be as perfect and unchanging as if he dwelt within a tomb. To that end, he had painted over those of his windows that offered only mediocre views, and in one instance had actually contracted for a stain glass pane of Tristan and Isolde to be built for his cottage. An attractive artifact, it scintillated with special beauty at the summer solstice and immediately adjacent days.

He had a telescope in fixed position, a half-dozen semi-domesticated pet raccoons, and a trove of alcoholic beverages. Had other things, including the normal pots and pans, drinking vessels, a .357 magnum eight-shot Smith & Wesson, and, at great expense, a battery driven water purification distillery fed from the nearby creek. Had nine dark suits of various weight and shades of blue. He also owned a supply of mysterious-looking ties ordered from the Duchamp Company in London, England. Dressed thus, no one bothered him or suspected the sort of person that he was.

These expensive foibles of his have led some to think he enjoyed a level of prosperity that in fact was very far from his real means. He had a pension and two rather trivial federal benefits that added up to somewhere between nineteen and twenty-one thousand dollars a year. Meanwhile, the house was fully owned, his diet was simple, and he had enough suits, ties, shoes, and books to last him till the end. His major expense by far was his monthly electricity bill, an obligation that stayed about the same whether it were hot or cold, or even whether he had been at home during the time. His smallest expense, by contrast, comprised the small sums he sometimes handed off to the tramps and "wayfarers" (he called them) who found a way to his door at a rate of about one-and-a-half per month.

Finally, he owned 240 acres of Alabama land, by far his proudest resource which however incurred a tax that sent him to the courthouse each year to argue over the amount.

"You surprise me Dr. Pefley," the lady always said. "We have the lowest taxes in the state!"

"Don't see how it could surprise you. I come here every year."

"That's true." And then, as if to change the conversation: "Oh! I like that tie!"

"Should. Cost me plenty."

"Enough to pay your taxes?"

Head held high, he exited the place in dignity. It was that time in the month when he must visit the grocery, a down-and-out sort of place patronized mostly by negroes and widows and thrifty people generally. Not that the food was cheaper here (quite the contrary!) but rather that he preferred the poverty and the inadequate lighting that had set up a cave-like ambience. Standing off to one side, he would watch the shoppers comparing prices, a tedious procedure that always seemed to leave them disappointed.

A woman had picked up a can of peas and after scrutinizing the rather short text that described the contents, immediately put it back. His attention then turned to yet another woman who had gathered up a piece of packaged meat, a liver or a gizzard or something of that kind, and seemed to be considering whether to purloin it or not. Lee looked at her severely, putting an end to the crime.

Himself, he was primarily interested in the foreign food section where sometimes he found products he had never tasted before. Using his pencil-size flashlight, he scanned the small array of anchovies and sardines, delighted by the curious little bright-colored labels that showed seascapes and coastal towns, exactly the sort of places he had imagined he might visit someday. His attention was called to a bottle of knurled pickles with the picture on it of the king of that place. Coming closer he ascertained that the man, dead these many years, had been about as decadent as one could wish, judging from him and his lidded expression.

Still moving forward, Lee then selected a jar of tiny little onions preserved in a syrup of some kind. In this case, the label bore the image of a crenellated tower with archers on guard, a medieval scene in which a smiling whale could be seen breaching the surface at a distance of perhaps half a mile from shore. As for wine (he had passed by now into that part of the store), the labels were almost as good. He saw a man and wife stomping grapes, and then a mule-drawn cart transporting the casks toward the presumed cellar where it would be turned into wine. He selected this bottle and then gathered up a cake of dark brown bread from Germany.

It was still light when he stepped out into the town and proceeded in a westerly direction. Soon now the shops would have closed, the working population would be trekking homeward while others, the worst in town, would be seen loitering about the taverns. Lee put on speed. The last he wanted was to stumble in among these types and have to put up with their insults. Too late.

"Hey! Buy me a drink professor, you want to?"

Lee grinned cordially. "I reckon not." And then: "I'd rather just give you the money, all right?"

"He'll give us the money, but he don't want to be seen with us—is that how it works? Hey, what you carrying in that big ole brown paper bag? That's what I want to know."

"Groceries."

"My wife usually does that."

"Wife? He hadn't got no wife. Shit, she done run off and left him long time ago!"

Lee grinned. His wife, it is true, had not been seen abroad for several months. Two further persons had come up and taken their place in front of the tavern door, giving him the chance to slip away in the crowd. Never slowing, he passed a department store preparing for Christmas a good six weeks before the event.

By 5:30, he had pretty well left the town behind and was moving in a western direction with his burden. It was the fluids, the milk and brandy, that weighed him down. He would have given a good deal to own a car with gasoline in it, and yet when one of the townsmen slowed and offered to carry him, Lee turned the invitation down.

"Much obliged," he said. "But I don't have much further to go."

"Yeah, I figured you'd say that. About two miles is all. Come on, get in."

Lee smiled in friendly fashion. "No, actually I need the exercise."

"Jesus." (He was a not-unkindly but also a primitive man who would expect Lee to talk of football, weather, women, and the price of things.) "What, you don't trust people like me? We're just regular folks."

"Yes. I think you've put your finger on it."

"Jesus!"

Lee strode to the truck and, his tact in temporary suspension, peered inside it. Empty paint cans, fence posts, a wooden keg with ice and beer in it—he couldn't count the times he had seen this syndrome among his local townsmen. No books.

"'Regular folk.' But imagine you had a magical little X-ray machine and could see what people *really* are?"

"I don't need no stinking machine!"

This proved the moment they departed, one man going off in one direction, and another the other. Night was moving in, and a keen person could almost perceive the atmospheric molecules mutating one by one to expose their darker selves. Lee, as keen a person as ever was, looked forward to the moment when the customary ugliness of things would be blotted out by night. (He had his way, and the sun would linger in the sky but for an hour or two, time enough for a gaudy dawn and not much else.) Meantime, it was getting chillier and him without a jacket. All his life it had been like this, the weather changing, his clothing badly chosen, a pebble in his shoe. Nor could he easily light a cigarette, not with his better arm committed to the groceries. And that of course was when a dog came up out of nowhere and after yapping at Lee briefly, turned his notice to the bag that Lee with increasing exasperation was still struggling to carry.

By 6:40, he had forded Drover's Creek and was moving forward noiselessly on the pine needle floor of the forest. He heard: 1) an owl blaring nearby, 2) autumn's last crickets, 3) hogs grunting in the distance. It was a pretty good time for him, his nerves were under control, and the night had come just in time to shield him from the occasional automobiles running down the highway. Furthermore, the moon was weak and the stars, all save one, more or less invisible. He could imagine that he was the only person left on earth, a time to forget about human things and turn his attention rather to the hills and trees and velvet black night itself; instead, he began looking about for a landmark place where he could store his milk and brandy and serotonin reuptake inhibitors to come back for them later on.

He entered his well-built home at a few minutes past eight and stood for a moment just inside the door lest someone might be lurking in the gloom. He had long ago eschewed artificial lighting in favor of the several kerosene lamps that had come down to him. Right away, strange silhouettes manifested on the walls, horses galloping down the hall, people murdering each other with knives, etc. Proceeding to the bedroom, he disarmed the shotgun pointed at the door and then, holding the lantern aslant, verified that his wife was resting comfortably. For him, the thoughts and wishes that once had occupied her cubic foot of grey matter were the *only things that had ever truly mattered,* an attitude that in his old age had left him unafraid of everything.

Lately, he had been reading in Teubner's new offering of Bacchylides' remains from Oxyrhynchus, a variorum edition that included the famous scholium mentioned in *Suda,* and when he checked, he found the book was as it ought to be, which is to say lying face-down at page 146. No one had entered the room; he was certain of it.

He made a short meal out of humus and cheese and washed it down with the remnant of white wine left over from last week. He had been thinking so hard and seriously in recent days, he felt the interior of his skull must look like a blast furnace. Soon now, would come the raccoons, dependencies of his addicted to the bits and pieces of cornbread distributed to them from the porch. Not that they were grateful! No, they seemed to think he was a fool making the same mistake each and every night. And in short, it was a leftover habit from his wife who used to leave crumbs for the flies.

He built a fire and then, acknowledging that he didn't really need one, snuffed it out again. Here in Alabama, the year had a great many days and nights, and yet only very few of them really required a fire. Up until this time he had been reasonably cheerful about this day and its routine contents, but not now, not with the wind beginning to behave more excitedly and the forest giving off the sound of animals suffering from nightmares. Winter was coming in.

They gathered, as always, the raccoons who graciously allowed the man to feed them. Except on this occasion a lemur (or something of that kind) had mixed in with the crowd and was striving to make herself as unnoticeable as possible. Suddenly, it occurred to Lee that he had not checked his mailbox for the past four days and that something good might be waiting for him, a letter perchance, his fishing magazine, a tax refund, or lottery winnings. Venturing out into the black night (the box was a good hundred rods from his domicile), he stood back and opened the thing at arm's length in case someone (and it wouldn't be the first time) had put a snake in it. No. No, there were only the usual advertisements, valuable documents that served as his best index to the deterioration taking place in the outer world.

Pleased, he hastened back to his well-constructed home and, pouring the last of the buttermilk, scanned with malevolent intent the first of the ads, a brightly-colored brochure promoting nasty underwear. Next, he was advised to purchase a certain form of liability insurance in the event a person was injured while trying to break into his house. "Hmm," he said, "I must have some of that. But does it cover shotgun blasts?" Finally, it was recommended that he order an electronic device whose function he wasn't able to discover. It had to do, he believed, with the ability to connect with yet other devices, one for each ear, having to do with expediting communications with other human beings. He snorted and laughed and then threw the sheet into the stove where right away it caught fire from the residual coals still lurking there.

The remaining documents he put within the ancient leather briefcase used by him during that brief effort to sell magazine subscriptions. Already three-fourths full, he aspired to bequeath these ads and menus, these coupons and application forms to some younger man, the new al-Juvaini perchance who in after times might come to be the essential historian of these times.

Two

For a long time, he had been wanting to get him down to the Gulf of Mexico. The weather was good, pretty good, and he wanted to take a final look at the blue-green sea. Pursuant to that, and because he needed to reinforce his equipment, he tiptoed down to the shed and after fuddling around for a long time with the frozen lock, gathered up his grandfather's fishing tackle box. There were some strange things in there, as he already knew, and he wasn't at all nonplussed by the some twenty dollars in coinage the old man had secreted in this place. As always, he checked the imprint dates and right away uncovered a dime minted in 1903, the same good year in which his grandfather's son had come into being. Of course, he saved that memento, Lee, depositing it along with his watch and chain in what was by far the deepest of his various pockets.

Even more incongruous than that, he found a few written pages and then a clumsy-looking fishing lure his ancestor had carved out of sycamore. The hook had broken off, but not before, Lee assumed, the artificer had probably caught all manner of fish with so rustic and so homemade a thing as that. Lifting it from the box, Lee inspected it more closely. Endowed with a human face, it portrayed a man with a beard and a sardonic expression.

The box, too, was of sycamore, Leland's second-favorite wood, and after so many years in storage was in a sorry state. He would have to replace one of the hinges, no doubt about that, and the whole thing would need to be bound up in cord to prevent it falling apart. He hefted it to his waist (damn thing was heavy) and carried it quickly to the kitchen where he dumped the contents on the floor. The odor was of salt water, a detail that pleased him beyond all proportion, knowing as he did that it denoted his grandfather's time at that selfsame Gulf of Mexico that his family had been patronizing for the past hundred years.

He discovered that his father had also made use of this equipage, judging from the flask, the fishing license (42 years out of date), and a certain membership card that had been soaking all this time in a puddle of oil mixed with brine. Lee held the thing to the light, hoping to learn more about his father's old-time attitudes and affiliations that for the most part had now also become his own. And then finally, a much-faded photograph of a pretty girl—where was she now?—wearing a bathing suit congruent with the styles of those times.

She had evidently been a fine person with good legs and bosoms, and Leland immediately found himself in danger of falling in love with her himself. For if the 1950s had been even just one part as lovely as he remembered, he could well imagine how things must have been twenty years earlier than that—beauty on top of beauty cumulating all the way back to Trojan Helen and her kind—such was his opinion of the effects of modernity upon women and girls.

He sought about for his glasses and then, working tediously in the afternoon light, reorganized everything that box contained. The license and membership cards—there were three—he placed together in one of the compartments that almost seemed to have been engineered for the purpose. As for the lures, he tried at first to arrange them by size and color, but then shortly gave up the effort and arrayed them alphabetically, placing each on its left side and vouchsafing each its own niche. No other improvements were made, apart from a twelve-inch butcher knife disguised in an oily rag.

Initially, it had been his scheme to set forth the following day; instead, seeing that the sun was wasting quickly, he went out into the exiguous light and, to save stress on his poor plumbing, urinated thoughtfully into his well-carved Halloween pumpkin that no one, insofar as he knew, had bothered to notice. Other pumpkins lay in other places among the cucumbers and roses that he had neglected to harvest. There was no doubt but that he had devoted too much attention to these matters, doing so more out of a sense of tradition than of need, and because he felt sometimes that his ancestors were looking down upon him from out of the sky.

Not so long ago, he had handed off his automobile, a 1947 Hudson Commodore 4-Door with six cylinders, to a naïve car collector willing to take it in exchange for a younger 1949 sea-green Fraser with a Continental Red Seal 226 CID "Supersonic" L-head six power plant. Retreating to the garage, he approached the car stealthily from long range, activated his battery recharger, and then jumped back out of range. He decided to use this time for loading his rods and tackle, a few tools, and jar of anti-freeze. He packed three days' worth of underwear and four suits, including a grey pin-stripe affair purchased two years ago at moderate cost from an Episcopal charity in Birmingham. Of ties, he liked to have about him more than just the three or four he might actually use; in fact, he liked to have about him as many as a dozen whenever he went on one of his "expeditions," as he called them. His shoes, on the other hand, or other foot rather (he snorted at the joke), were in deleterious condition and would shortly need to be repaired. His cufflinks by contrast were of the very best, and in three out of four cases were engraved with the profiles of Greek heroes and even gods indeed.

His money. He had decided to take two thousand dollars, not including the coinage in his grandfather's tackle box. Returning to the house, he took down a somewhat tatty copy of Galen's medicine and opened it to the place where he stored his larger bills. The money was still there, also a crushed flower that related to an experience of some fifty years ago—he tried not to think about that. Realizing almost too late that he had forgotten his pills and alcohol, he retrieved a bottle of pre-mixed daiquiri, a pint of brandy, and a hefty container of strengthened eggnog left over from last Christmas. Came next the pills—three several kinds of serotonin reuptake inhibitors made up of some of the most ingenious molecules in the entire pharmacopeia. (He took one of these pills on the spot and waited for it to metabolize.)

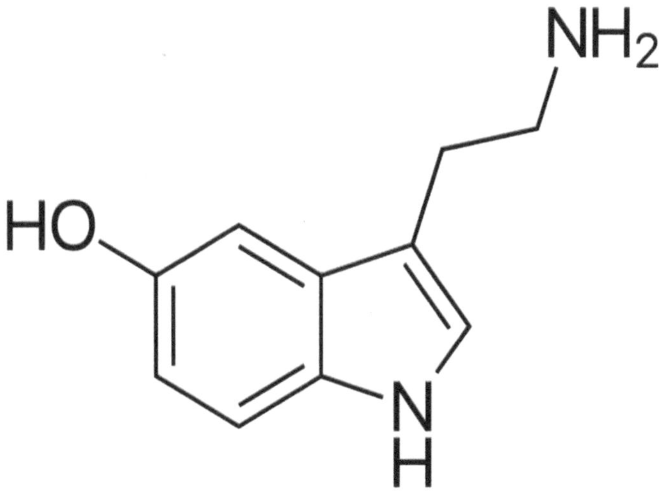

He chose four books and then, to make certain he wouldn't run out of reading material, four more. He could read no word of Persian, and yet he hated to be without the most beautiful codex in his collection, an ornate production in purple and gold printed in an insidious script that looked like whispering. He took volume nine of Rosenthal's aforementioned *al-Tabari*, even though he hadn't done volume two as yet. He took two Roman histories, intending to stage a competition between them. And of course, a cellophane-covered copy of *The New Austerities*, a much-impugned masterpiece written by its author.

He had hoped that the battery in his Fraser had been fully energized by now wherefore he reported back to the garage and inserted the key. It was a heavy and obsolete-looking thing, that key, and he had to use both hands to cause it to turn in the socket. Despair came down on him when the car merely trembled once or twice and gave off the unmistakable sound of alarmed mice—apparently, they had been dwelling in the engine works—of mice scurrying for safety. They could chew through anything, could mice, but had they actually devoured his motor? Had they, for example, been sipping at the gasoline, or perchance had blocked the hoses with their stools? He thought not, no, and so again he tried the key which this time wouldn't turn at all. "Goddamn it!" he said, recognizing belatedly that he had been using his Hudson key. He went on: "Now this time I'm going to use my *Fraser* key by God!"

All his life, he had preferred his manufactured products to have been built before 1949. Using the proper key, he now tested the power beneath the hood, the engineering that had gone into the thing, and the hearty sound of old-time music on the radio. The brakes were fine, too, and he was able to drive the vehicle in any direction without concern. It is true that he had forgotten the layout of the gears, though this, too, soon came back to him as he ran through the permutations.

Twice he drove about the house, testing the steering and the radio and the half-dozen little indicator lights that blinked and gleamed in the way he remembered from other cars and earlier expeditions. It was not an unimportant feature in his opinion, that these dials be illuminated in deep purple and cerulean blue as opposed, for example, to the lightweight colors preferred by modern people. And when he looked into the mirror, lo, it exposed a considerable swatch of his own archaic face illuminated by the moon.

Finally, he went back to the well-constructed house and did the other things: loaded his shotgun with fresh ammunition, shut down the water and electricity, and strewed the back yard with four days of fodder for the lemurs. Of his wife, he did the usual things that were done whenever he was setting out on a long and difficult journey with no imperative purpose in mind.

Three

He drove forward into the gloaming. It is true that his front lights were sputtering badly, giving only intermittent views of the road coming up much too quickly for a person of his deteriorated vision. He passed a roadside sign foretelling of a restaurant up ahead. He slowed, passing a hay wagon that had chosen this irrational hour to be out and abroad. Irrational? No, the fellow was simply trying to avoid the late afternoon traffic.

He was quite calm, able still to recognize himself in the mirror as that same "craggy" sort of individual with a "spiritual air," as ascribed to him when he was twenty. His cigarette was powerful, and he was conscious of his liquor, his books, his pharmaceutical reserves, and double-barrel shotgun. Dithering with the radio, he honed in on the haunting voice of "The Velvet Fog," as the man had been denominated in his day. Lee slowed for it, waiting till the final chord before returning to normal speed. He had been wise to settle upon an early vintage car with a radio of this kind, not to mention a dashboard with so many mysterious blue and purple lights. Came then *Why Don't You Believe Me?,* the best single example of the work of Patti Page, last heard by Lee in 1952 while dancing with the third-most beautiful girl in school.

The road was long and narrow and the roadside advertisements among the finest he had ever seen. He rushed past a broken-down billboard promoting a luxurious hotel that as he knew for a fact no longer existed. As for the directional signposts, they seemed to point off in all sorts of directions and even to contradict each other on occasion. He was far from Tallahassee, but already they were discussing the number of miles yet to go. He hated the attention given to big cities and was about to say something about it when just that moment he broke into the edge of a tiny village called *Washington*, named, it was said, after one of the nephews of the nation's first president.

The place had but one street of any size, and it was laden on both sides with two-and three-story homes betokening the town's prosperity. Lee slowed. The people, prudent and good, had brought inside their bicycles, had latched their latches, and by 7:00 were dreaming wholesome dreams between clean sheets. How he did envy them, he who had ruined his life with too much education and too much time in cities! Just then, a man with a large brown dog on a string called out the hour and then turned on his heel and walked back in his traces. Lee counted the tolling of the bell, counting up to seven and not one moment more. Each porch had a dog on it, suspicious creatures of a pessimistic cast.

Lee "tiptoed" out of town, figuratively speaking, and ran for about three, possibly four miles before coming abreast with the all-night restaurant advertised above. The place was wreathed in strings of neon Christmas lighting—he liked that part—but also had a good number of automobiles and motorcycles arrayed—he didn't like this at all—in disorderly fashion about the lot. Nevertheless, he came and parked and tried to remember how to turn off the lights and ignition and open the door on his side. The very last he wanted was a gathering of hoodlums drinking beer, the sort as might make fun of his car and his age, his costume, and the admittedly rather thick volume he had chosen to bring. To be sure, he also carried a .357 caliber eight-shot Smith & Wesson that might or might not have cartridges enough for the whole crew.

He entered but then came out again as soon as he had been assaulted by the music they were playing. They should be made to wear little yellow pointed hats, Lee believed, those who listened to such God-awful stuff. Torn between the smell of coffee and hamburgers on the one hand, and "music" on the other, he did enter after all and after waiting for his eyes to adapt, trundled inconspicuously, as he believed, toward the far end of the building, (formerly a barn) while looking down at the floor. His one chance was that the old Southern tradition of respect for aged people still applied. Putting on an expression rilled with sorrow and old age, he sat quietly beneath the framed portrait of an African basketball player whose antediluvian face was yet more problematic than Lee's.

He had started to ask for a simple cheeseburger but changed his mind when he saw they were offering poached river eels in a buttermilk sauce. He alit upon this item right away, at the same time adding a mug of the local beer. His suit was newly pressed, and his tie bore iridescent images of fantail peacocks with their feathers all aglitter. As to the waitress, she proved to be a tired-looking quantity who, although not probably a whore, had long ago sacrificed many of the principles urged by her mother—this was Lee's impression of the person.

"And hot biscuits, too, please," he asked in the shy way he had developed in his continuing effort to get along better with people.

She wrote it down. Her pencil was short, her dress askew, and her breasts pointed off in quite different directions. He experienced a sudden unwonted sympathy for her—a girl who had dropped to earth some thirty-six years ago in the expectation of all sorts of good things. Looking steadily at her, Lee divined that although she had perhaps been penetrated often enough, nothing else had come her way.

"And marmalade, too, please? To go with the biscuits?"

She wrote it down. She had a contusion on her neck where her loutish boyfriend had been sucking on her.

"You worked here a long time?" he asked.

"Sir? No, about three months is all."

"I see. Actually, I'd be willing to pay the tuition, some of it anyway, if you decided to get some training. Radiology, dental assistant, something like that."

She paled and backed off three paces. "No, sir, I've already got a job. But thank you anyway; that's real nice."

He could expect to be ejected from the restaurant; the girl had gone to a large man at the bar and the two of them were looking back with serious disapproval. He turned his attention, Leland, to three burly men—they had rather have their toes removed than to read a good book—three burly ones placing bets at the pinball machine. Three other men had come together at a table near Lee's and were whispering audibly of women, tax evasion, gas mileage, and bowling scores. Using his powers, Lee saw that the fattest of them was already infected with the malady that was to kill him within a few months. And now at this late date, what, really, did he still want? Free beer and televised hockey games with narrow scores? But the evening could not be *absolutely* perfect until he had overheard a bourgeois family speaking excitedly about a forthcoming rock concert, a conversation that followed hard upon.

He wanted to slay the lot of them. They had been traveling down the road of life and had opted for the manure on one side while staying oblivious to the gold on the other. Meantime, the man at the bar was still looking at him. Lifting his tankard of beer, Lee quaffed off perhaps three fluid ounces of the stuff and then set it down in a shallow puddle (about a twentieth inch) of condensation. How he hated these unnecessary and pestilential flaws of nature—condensation, mildew and rust, broken pipes, all of it! That was when the galoot at the bar pushed off and sauntered toward him. Hurrying to finish the beer before being expelled, Lee smiled at him through the thick and somewhat lens-like glass at the bottom of the mug.

"We don't take too kindly to people like you," the galoot revealed.

"I know."

"Messing around with waitresses for God's sakes. Anyway, you're too old for that."

"I *am* old."

"Okay, tell you what, you take that there beer and go spill it somewhere else, okay?"

"I haven't even paid for it yet! Besides, it's only condensation."

"And I won't charge you nothing either, okay? Now you can't ask for better than that, right? Nobody can."

Lee had to agree. In the kitchen he could see his eels under preparation and the look of disgust on the face of the chef.

He carried the beer with him and after finishing it, stored the mug in the back seat of the Fraser along with his other possessions. He had entered the establishment with some two thousand dollars on his person and except for a rather trivial tip, had left with the same sum exactly. The car and he, adjusted for life expectancy, were of about the same age, and both of them seemed to be suffering from the same sort of gastritis, if that's the best word for what was happening beneath the hood. Two miles out he gained on a hitchhiker and was actually about to stop, which is to say until he got a better view of the individual's face. He did *not* want to be set upon, robbed, and mutilated, his car taken over by a weathered-looking boy with tattoos on him. He did have a powerful arm, the boy, and the stone he threw came down a good half-dozen yards *in advance* of Leland's car. He put on speed, Lee, or tried to. The highway was not a recent creation and was just about obsolete for all but mules and tractors and the sort.

Followed then a certain amount of time during which Lee was more or less unconscious. Nothing was more relaxing to him than to be bouncing though time and history with forests on both sides. He passed a tumble-down cottage, the windows full of faces. Ran over a congealed creek colored blood-red. Nor was he unaware of the buzzard, or outsized crow flying in tandem with him and, sometimes, turning to peep at him from about six inches away. He expected it. Never yet had he been able to drive through the Alabama night without anomalies of various kind presenting themselves to his face. Far away, a radio tower was flashing erratically while emitting messages to Central and South America and points even further than that. And all this time the clouds congregating east and west. He saw, he thought, thought Lee, a tribe of archaic humans hiking across the field, but then came awake just in time to keep from running off the road and into a growth of unharvested beans.

It was almost nine o'clock by this time, and he had gone about seventeen miles, judging from the meter. He had long ago left behind the acreage familiar to him from boyhood and seemed to be entering a flora and a topography that differed perceptibly from his natal lands. He didn't like it. Where, for example, was the quota of Spanish Moss, the road lizards, and the other "furniture" that he had assumed must always be present wherever he might go? Instead, they had set up in this place a tiny village with a Dutch windmill for the tourists—he wanted to vomit.

In a town like this one, he needed no time at all to find a service station with three picturesque negroes positioned about the pump. Lee ran past the place, but then turned and came back and, ignoring the laughter that his car always inspired, rolled down the window and spoke with the most formidable-looking of the black people.

"Doing any good?" Leland asked.

"Not too bad. Had some people from New Jersey a little while back." (He had a ten-dollar bill sticking from his shirt pocket.)

"Good. That's real good. But you need to wear a torn shirt, like you've just been whipped."

"Whoa! You the man!"

There were other negroes inside the windmill, not to mention a very mournful-looking restroom attendant of about seventy years. Lee peed, at the same time allowing the man to approach from about twenty feet away and begin to brush and floss Leland's high-priced jacket. They looked at each other in the mirror. Unable to go on with it under these conditions, Lee closed down what he was doing and waited, quite uselessly, for the fellow to go away. He could pee and pay, or *not* pay and do without peeing.

"How much?"

"Yas, suh. Dolla be good."

Forever naïve, Lee paid with a five-dollar bill and then waited, again fruitlessly, for at least some bit of change to come back to him. He could hear a small tittering from one of the cells where two high-heel shoes were sticking out. A thousand years might go by, but never would Lee understand these modern concepts of romance, an egalitarian movement that enraged the few remaining decent people everywhere.

Walking backwards to deceive the CCTV camera peeping from a stuffed raven just above the chamber door, he exited the room with dignity and after zipping up his fly on the fly and continued on foot to a cozy little boutique designed for people of the arts and crafts sort. Here, for a remarkable price, a person could invest in little containers of honey shaped like the Taj Mahal or, depending upon the tourist, framed portraits of Martin Luther King, Jr. gazing off into the stars. One could buy a package of grits in a brown bag with the picture of a stern-looking farmer on it. One could acquire a bundle of post cards wrapped in cellophane, each card showing a different perspective of Myrtle Beach. Or, one might prefer a little pink plastic mermaid with bosoms that seemed out of sync with her size and weight. Taking up a stance in the middle of the store, Lee now spoke to himself in the privacy of his diffidence, saying: "No, really I need to be more tolerant of people and places, yea and institutions, too. God knows I've tried."

He had not tried, or not with any consistency at any rate, this man who had locked himself away in a cabin along with his quiescent wife. "No, the truth is that . . ." (He was talking again, talking again to his own self alone.) "No, the truth is that I have indulged myself far too long in the most addictive avocation of all, called '*thought*.' God knows I've tried to stop."

He had not tried to stop, certainly not now with a crowd of numskulls pushing their way into the shop and scattering to the various counters. All were talking at the same time, all were smiling, all had money enough and to spare—history's most cheerful and healthy and most solvent youths; he wanted to vomit. (As one who adored civilization, he had come to abhor the majority of its ingredients. That's just how he was.) Wishing to increase the distance between he and them, Lee edged to the magazine rack where he determined that a full 62% of the journals displayed colored photographs of undressed girls suffering, apparently, from a self-inflicted starvation of some nature, a ghastly sight that caused him to jump back two paces before then returning to the scene and scrutinizing at close range the girls' very wicked facial expressions, the result, he felt sure, of a great deal of practice behind closed doors. A hundred years ago it would have been unsullied girls in crinoline and lace, before the expectations of males had been through a "paradigm shift," as advanced people were prone to say.

Shifting his attention from the journals to living girls, he noticed in particular a fifteen- or perhaps sixteen-year-old with much powder on her face and eyes fixed up like Cleopatra's. What did she want really, to experience the male organ moving in and out of one or another of her orifices? Is that what it comes to, just that? Why not a cucumber or writing quill, and why not her ear in place of her birthing canal? By God, he hated the baseness of things and people, the stink of human flesh, the pus and blood, lymph and piss, saliva and snot, and all the other recrements that must have been just as degrading and as unavoidable among the Greeks as among post-modern decadents.

Truth was, they would do just about anything, girls, to get the notice they thirsted for. Would they for example… Suddenly he jumped back, pushed by the crowd toward the far end of the building. For example, would they go about with human scalps dangling from their hats? Bet your ass they would.

He came out and supported himself for a while against the wall, waiting for his mind to recover. The night was turning chill, and the stars were beginning to shudder very slightly, each shudder ten thousand years. Already he was lost in time and space (time especially), and he could not altogether understand how he had ended up in a place like this, a nighttime emporium somewhere along a highway in south-central Alabama. That was when he spied someone trying to force open his car.

Lee ran to the spot, but then slowed when he saw the person's size. Putting on a neighborly expression, he spoke this way:

"Howdy! Yep, I reckon that old car is just about as old as me!"

Slowly the man, or boy rather, withdrew his head from the window and fixed his eyes on Lee. He was a chapped and rubicund sort of person, roseate and gimlet-eyed and dressed in a T-shirt tailored to show off his pectorals. It was clear that he had endured some very serious surgery recently, but not enough to make him *truly* look like Elvis. He spoke in a soft tone situated halfway between courtesy and disgust.

"I've read about these," he said. "But I ain't never seen one."

"Well, that's what happens when you read too much."

"Naw, shit, I'm talking about the *car,* not you. Want to sell it?"

"I've *always* wanted to sell it. And so would you." He laughed cordially, albeit without accompaniment.

"Give you . . ."

Lee waited for it.

"Three hundred?"

Lee jumped back. He was transporting that much in his left shoe alone. "I reckon not."

"Say what?"

"No, thanks."

"The shit! I come here, I make you a good offer. I guess you just aren't too damn friendly, are you?"

The .32 caliber revolver was beneath the driver's seat, the .357 even further. Lee then tried to shake with him. "I'll take three thousand for it."

"I reckon you would! Shit. I come here, I make a good offer. What, you some kind of *Jew*, or something?"

"Ha! No, no, I just . . ."

Came then another boy, or man rather, this one a florid, amaranthine type of an aubergine coloration dressed in a cummerbund and a sprig of eglantine in his lapel.

"He bothering you?"

"Little bit," said Lee.

"Hey! I ain't talking to you, I'm talking to *him*!"

"Little bit," said the roseate man.

"And what kind of car is that anyway?"

"Actually, I was just leaving. And besides, you can see how old I am."

"He *is* old."

"I don't know. Sometimes they're the worst."

"That's true," Lee agreed. "Me, I knew this old boy who lived over in . . ."

"Talladega?"

"Why yes."

"Tell you what, why don't you just climb back inside this . . . whatever the hell it is, and head on out of here? Hm?"

"Yeah," said Lee thoughtfully. "I'm thinking maybe I ought to just climb back into this . . . And head on out of here!"

Pleased to have reached this accommodation, the three men shook all around. From the restaurant one could hear some very primitive music that seemed to form a backdrop to the sight and the smell of yet another town going up in flame at a distance of about twenty miles.

He drove on, drove Leland, in a disconsolate frame of mind. His inherent nature urged him to turn and go back and have it out with the two large malefactors who had treated him that way. However, having decided like one of his literary heroes, that courage was the inferior part of prudence, he continued on. He was picking up some strange noises from under the hood of his car, as also from his belly crying out for food. Too, he was listening to an advertisement on the radio, a song-and-dance number related to a brand of toothpaste. And then finally, as if all the above were not enough, the very late autumn crickets were causing themselves to be heard through the portholes of his antiquarian car.

There were other sounds and other smells, the result, most of them, of his too active imagination. Because this is what it's like for a man of his type—to be dreaming about the funeral rites of Hector while at the same time probing into townships and counties never seen before. He dashed past a deserted farmstead that reminded him of Boeotia, and then a radio tower (set with three green lamps) that impaled the world. He called up in mind a saying of Wordsworth's, and then required himself to conjugate a certain German verb. And in short, his mind was like a beehive assailed by bears.

All this passed away, however, when the radio began to play some of the romantic ballads of his own day—the school of Billy Eckstine and Patti Page. He drifted this way and that, and then, sure enough, the next he knew he was dancing with the second-prettiest girl in school. And if he couldn't entirely remember her face, he could recall her yellow gown and uncanny perfume that lingered with him still.

He refused to cry. Instead, he pulled over onto the shoulder and, taking out his field glasses, tried to situate himself with regard to the assumed landmarks—there were not any—that he had hoped would point the way to Florida. As noted, there were no landmarks anywhere, a dismaying development that resorted him to the maps in his glove compartment. Somehow, he had acquired a brightly colored chart showing some of the more memorable spots in Saxon England, useless to him at this juncture. His Barretta, to be sure, was as it should be, as also the two packs of Egyptian cigarettes that nowadays could not be used in population centers. Looking about carefully, he actually lit up one of those cigarettes and quickly smoked it down to a length of perhaps two inches before another car happened along.

He had a pair of socks in the same compartment as, too, a bottle of whiskey that had almost entirely evaporated during the last half-century. He had a tire pressure gauge, a pencil, a snake bite kit, a dozen shells of ammunition, and a stamp-size engraving of Nathan Forrest in a golden locket. The map he sought dated from 1950 and displayed the whole state at the very best moment in his and Alabama's whole career.

He refused to cry. He still had a few years in front of him, time enough to do some heavy thinking and, relying upon the power of thought and will, to change the course of modern history. Not likely. And besides, his *true* desire, the one that pushed him into dangerous expedients, his *real* desire, as he started to say, was to slice open the transparent sarcophagus in which his wife was sleeping and place himself at her side.

Four

He drove on through the manifold night. The stars had thinned out but at the same time had become more active. Using his binoculars, he honed in on what was perhaps the least obvious of them all, a ragged manifestation steadfastly turning helium back to hydrogen, as he mooted to himself humorously. Suddenly (and this was the second time), he ran off the highway and proceeded at high speed for about fifty yards through high weeds before correcting himself.

Someone had left a dead opossum in the middle of the road, and Lee, striving to avoid it, ran over a portion of it.

It encouraged him at long last to put on his double-glazed glasses, a heavy appliance that compressed his nose and made it difficult to go on breathing. Not that he cared so greatly about breathing! On the contrary he saw it as just one more physiological inconvenience, along with locomotion and the circulation of the blood.

He was thinking again. The most awful of all habits, he often wished he could return to the springtime of his life, the embryonic stage where, as he well remembered, he had never thought at all. Or even just to be five years old again and riding silently by night in the back of the family car. Or eleven, and dancing with any single one of the twenty or thirty beauties he had known. Or all of them at once. Or eighteen, and running insanely through a downpour of cold rain. Or heck, to be forty once more and in possession of a body that still functioned passably well almost all the time.

Instead, he was an old man, desiccated and bleak, his nose a halberd for slicing through the night. As for his legs, they looked like stilts dangling from a pair of too-large pantaloons. His arms, meantime, were retreating into their sockets and retained no more than two or three years of usefulness at most. Saddened by this drear inventory, he now tried one more time not to think about anything at all.

His head was like an Aladdin's lamp and had a spout on it. Flitches of bacon were his feet, each of them splayed out into five unequal niblets. His fingers were ten, and three of them had been broken often enough to disturb anyone consenting to shake his hand. His resumé included also some five operations, a bout of pulmonary disease, and a "male hysterectomy," so-called by his team of jesting surgeons. He suffered both from old and pneumonia, glanders and mange, shingles and headaches. And if twice he had tried to carry out operations on himself . . . Never yet had he met anyone who wanted the details.

These were the reasons he had been prescribed seven different pharmaceutical medications, all of them contained in plastic bottles with child-proof caps that challenged what remained of his intelligence. With one hand on the wheel, another on the revolver, and his ear on the radio, his mind flitted back momentarily to 1952 and then came slowly forward to the present moment. Meantime, the car was gasping and would not last the night.

He took two pink pills, asterisk-shaped businesses that would *not* go down. "Goddamn it," he said softly without opening his mouth. To dislodge these nuisances, he took a swig of whiskey which right away caused the things to melt. Far more amenable were the white ones, wee things, quite tasteless, and of his favorite size.

It wasn't till 9:48 that another car came up alongside and, after examining the old man for a few seconds, passed him by. Lee, who resented people of this kind, put on speed. The fellow had a woman with him together with what either were two children, or one dog and one child. But at this point Leland's heart began to soften somewhat. Both had long tongues and, judging from their silhouettes, were viewing the unfolding countryside with greater attention than the adults. For them (dogs), life was interesting, and would forever be as long as hills and trees and cattle (cattle particularly) invested the astonishing world. Broaching up nearer to them, Lee read the two rather threatening bumper stickers that might almost have been put on display for his sole benefit alone. Coming still nearer, he was finally able to decipher the third message, which pertained to something having to do with the United Nations.

Just then, or slightly before, later, a motorcycle emerged out of the night and began the process of passing both cars. Incensed, Lee turned to see an impressive-looking male at the controls and behind him a pretty, in fact beautiful, female girl in (despite the weather) tight white shorts. They all looked at one another for a brief moment, which is to say till the cycle went into overdrive and fled out of sight down the road. This time it really did take Lee an effort to keep from bawling out loud. How long, pray, since last *he* had had a vehicle like that? Or more to the point, how long since a bare-legged girl in lipstick had held *him* about the waist, eyes aglow with excitement and contentment? "Never," he admitted at last, confessing the truth out loud for his own ears solely.

By 10:17 he had penetrated into a town named after perhaps the most celebrated artillery officer of The War Against the States. They had put up a statue, the townspeople had, of the man himself, a passionate revanchist who had spent his last sixteen years in Federal durance. Lee pulled over and got out, and after worming his way through a crowd of post-modern youths with ludicrous haircuts, strolled to the base of the sculpture and stood for a while. Had ever anyone striven harder or more persistently to ward away the sort of future here on view—a gathering of sneering seventeen-year-olds, their heads full of "music" and stupor and all sorts of other variegated shit?

He wanted to borrow the hero's sharp granite sword and slash the modern world to death. Wanted the bad half of humanity chained to the floor and then to find himself with a flame thrower. In fact, he had been on the road for two hours nearly and had covered not thirty-five miles as yet. Even so he was outrunning the reach of the old-fashioned radio station and was beginning to acquire more modern sounds, most of it performed by Hottentots yearning for the old continent. Just that moment, or a little earlier actually, he came to a branch in the road that offered a better highway than the one he was using. Of course, he had to ascertain whether it pointed in the proper direction, more or less, and would carry him to Florida. His flashlight, unfortunately, had burned down, and he had to leave the cockpit and go to the head of the car in order to read said map in the light of the left-side lamp.

Truly it was a superior road, smoother, less litter along the shoulders, and he was able to push the car to a somewhat better speed than heretofore. Came then an excited voice over the radio telling how magnesium exports had deteriorated over the past quarter. Sorghum was up but fundamentals were down—he wanted to weep. Meanwhile he was bearing down on an enormous tractor whose foolish driver was moving at about twenty miles the hour on this built-for-speed highway. Lee crawled nearer, critiquing the shape of the fellow's stubborn head. It didn't care, that head, that the ambient world wished to go faster. Lee now pulled abreast of the person and let the window down, saying:

"It's late, too late for you to be . . ."

"Where'd you get that car?" (His voice was parched, and he was wearing a pair of very tiny spectacles, the lenses not much larger, respectively speaking, than a nickel and a quarter.)

"I got this car," said Lee, pointing to it, "from a naïve man who seemed to believe . . ."

"What kind of man?"

"Naïve."

"Cheated him, didn't you? Cheated that good man."

"Little bit. Hey, where you going?"

(The farmer had put on what was probably his best speed and now was fleeing southwestwardly at perhaps twenty-five miles the hour. Lee had no difficulty catching up with him. Snout to snout, they blocked the highway, all save for a few inches on either side.)

"Of course, *you* never cheated, is that what you're claiming?"

"Bad for business."

"Yes, and if it were good for business, what then?"

But the man never answered. A third car had come down on them, the driver halting a few yards behind and offering help.

"You fellows need any help?" (He was a bland person, also very naïve as Lee divined. Well-dressed for the most part, he was wearing a despicable little bowtie whose color was not immediately identifiable in the dark black night.)

"Don't help *him*!" the farmer said. "He cheats."

"Just once," said Lee, his anger rising. "I tried to explain this to him."

The Samaritan looked back and forth at them, deciding finally upon the farmer as the more trustworthy.

"What, you need a battery charge?"

"Hell, no I don't need no charge! I always carry an extra one—see it sitting up there? Everybody knows that."

Reluctantly, the city boy now turned his attention upon Lee. "How about you?"

"Me? I never carry an extra one. Don't believe in it."

"Oh."

"This car," said Lee, getting out and patting the fender, "has near about 10,000 parts. And you want me to carry all that stuff around with me all the time? No, thanks."

"Well, if I could just get around you . . ."

Instead, that was when a fourth car arrived, this one navigated by a woman in a scarlet raincoat with a hood on it. Unable to make out what sort she was, Lee took his dysfunctional flashlight and shone it in her face.

"As if we didn't have problems enough," he said in courteous voice. "Why the raincoat?"

"Can I get by?"

Lee came closer, the woman very quickly winding up the window on that side. He had learned long ago to determine a woman's age by the condition of her neck. Suddenly he jumped back, nonplussed by the vision of a man slumped in the adjoining seat. Whether drunk, dead, or just sleeping, Lee wasn't ready to venture.

"Dead?"

"Maybe if you could just move that blue car . . ."

"Listen, we're doing the best we can! Christ."

Came now the farmer, who possessed a flashlight of his own. The woman's neck, as he was quickly able to discern, bespoke a certain age. "I always carry *two* flashlights," he said. "One over here and one over yonder."

"What about her husband?"

"Can't say. 'Bout forty years old, I reckon. Oh, oh, he's looking at us."

"You don't know that's her husband. Be honest."

By this time a fifth car had arrived. Seeing the mess up ahead, the driver suddenly turned very sharply and sped off precisely in the direction opposite to his original intent. Overhead, a platoon of crows had come to a stop in midair and seemed to be jeering at them.

"Besides, he was *happy* to be cheated," said Lee, facing his interlocutor who had come to his feet in such a way as to let it be seen that he was somewhat, if not tremendously, larger than the ordinary southern man. They were impressed by the woman who had actually managed to get past them by trespassing into the roadside ditch and then climbing out by aid of her 300-horsepower engine.

"She's going. Never see her again."

"Crazy, if he thinks he can do the same." (Lee was referring to the city man trying to follow in the woman's tracks.) "Shoot, he's stuck already!"

It was true that the farmer might be able to pull him out. Not so Lee, whose vehicle wasn't set up for projects of that kind. Meantime, the southbound lane, free of so much traffic, again was available to Lee.

He continued on for a goodly distance, never stopping till he came to an early-to-bed little town strewn with wooden shacks that continued up the hillside. Even here, he did not stop however, not till he was in open country once more, once more running between fields and cows and pastures and morose-looking gasoline stations closed for the night. He did so love the American highway system—he admitted it—and the great choice of roads going off in all directions. One might select one of those thoroughfares at random and end up several days later in some of the strangest places. Or he could focus, that person, upon the other automobiles with their pastel taillights, iridescent signifiers telling of doomed peoples locked away forever in their cars. Going nowhere! Himself, he had recognized an hour ago that he was moving in an eastwardly direction when all he had ever really wanted was to go to Florida. Came now an immense truck, a tremendous nocturnal beetle with fifteen lights all aglow. Lee slowed and let it pass, although his courtesy failed to dissuade the driver from releasing a spume of vapor precisely into Leland's face.

On the other hand, he was free here to light up a cigarette, provided he hide the thing in the cup of his hand whenever he passed a government official, or found himself in the rays of one of the overhead monitors mounted unpredictably along the highway. He had not had a smoke in forty minutes, nor listened to a single note of Mahler's or Wagner's in an even larger stretch of time. And then, too, he was getting sleepy, normally a daytime vice for him. He began humming loudly but could by no means simulate even approximately any of his favorite arias.

At 10:17 he rolled into the mediocre town of Alabama *Brenman,* so-named after a certain old-time duelist and politician. And when, pray, might he come upon a place called *Poe,* or even *Faulkner* indeed? It was a sodden place, Brenman, and the economy had done so poorly in recent years that taxes were payable either in specie, labor, or kind. It had rained here recently, reckoning from the puddles and the woman drifting down the street in an umbrella and raincoat. Taking up his field glasses, she looked to him like a reasonable person, but careworn, and wearing some make-up, though not enough. Populated mostly with a reclusive people, the town boasted a single grocery store and not much else. Estimating the town from this and its undoubted secrets—love, murder, etc.—he pulled in at a motel called also Brenman after that same famous person, he supposed.

Unfortunately, the woman at the desk was a minimally-interesting type altogether, a simple twenty-five- or thirty-year-old watching television with dulled eyes. Her mouth had lapsed open at some date, and she'd never found the wherewithal to close it up again. Continuing with it, Lee foresaw with his magic vision that she had a child but no spouse, and the child was staying with its grandmother. And this pathetic job, he foresaw clearly, was the best that she would ever have. Entering with dignity, Lee paused in the doorway that the girl could see what sort he was and how conscientiously dressed. That did it—she immediately came awake and put on a smile as warm and cheerful—Lee jumped back—as an encyclopedia salesman's.

"'Evening," he said. "I'm in the market for a place to stay tonight."

"Just the one of you?"

Lee looked behind him. "That's right, yes."

"You could have room . . ." (She was running down a list of rooms and numbers and hasty little sketches—his opinion of the girl improved—thumbnail sketches of the tenants.) ". . . 243."

"Sounds good. What's the fee?"

"That will be . . ." (Another list.) "$72.50."

"I'm sorry?"

"$72.50."

"Gad."

"Plus tax."

"My God. Last time I stayed in a place like this it was

nine dollars!"

"We don't have anything like that."

"Ah. It's just that I'm on a fixed income don't you see, and . . . $72.50?"

"Yes, sir."

"Boy howdy. I think maybe I ought to get a second opinion, so to speak. From one of these other places, if you don't mind."

"You could try *Prunty and Mullin's.* It they're still in business."

"*Prunty*, yes, I think I will, if you don't mind. Is there something wrong with them?"

But the girl was not taking any more questions. The television had run over into a commercial, calling her attention back to the screen.

He never had any intention of *Prunty*, or at least not until he could make himself understand what it was that caused *this* place to be so dear. Accordingly, he ran behind the building, which was long and narrow, and then had to go on for a full thirty or forty rods more before finding an uncovered window. There he saw an old man sitting on the edge of his bed suffering from what appeared to be indigestion. Lee perceived a few pieces of generic furniture, a television set, a briefcase, and on the table a substantial collection of toiletries (toothbrush, etc.) arrayed in order of need. Other than that, he saw nothing that merited $72.50, or even one-fourth that.

The following window had also an elderly man in it, this one lying face-up on the bed with his eyes three-fourths closed. What memories, what dreams, what appalling discouragements had not this one seen? Running his mind backward into the past, Lee could divine everything one needed to know about this person's ungrateful children, post-modern types making big salaries in Montgomery or Birmingham. Computer people with overdeveloped index fingers, he wanted to slay the lot of them.

It needed him half an hour, almost, to find *Prunty's* over by the loading dock. And even then, he couldn't be certain whether it were open for business or not. He drove past and then came back, pleased to see a tattered and, for him, highly nostalgic billboard promoting a brand of cornbread mix that he knew for a fact had gone out of existence many years ago. Here Leland parked and after waiting for the engine to shudder to a stop, took up his .357, and marched toward what appeared to be the business office. There were some people in there, but the window was so very cloudy that one could not easily say how many they were. Taking his courage, he suddenly burst into the room, realizing belatedly that he had forgot to tuck his revolver into its accustomed place. At the sight of that weapon the men (they were men), all jumped up together in wild surmise.

"Whoa!" one of them said. "He ain't here."

"Actually, I'm just looking for a place to spend the night, actually."

Two of the men sat down. They had been playing Chinese Checkers with yellow marbles, one of which was lying on the floor. They had been wagering large sums, reckoning by the cash on view.

"I wonder what the fee is?" mooted Lee.

"Well, he could sure tell you. If he was here."

"I see." Lee hummed. "Wonder if I could see one of the rooms?"

The standing man came closer. He was wearing a red velvet gilet and his hair was kept in place with oil.

"Now, why would you want to do that?" he asked. "And besides, which room you talking about?"

"Any of them."

"We don't have nothing like that."

"How about room 243?"

"243? He must be thinking about Bertrand's place."

Lee grinned apologetically and smote himself on the forehead.

"Yes! In fact, I *was* thinking about that other place! Stupid, stupid!"

"And another thing, how come you wearing them Sunday clothes?"

Said another: "Aw, I don't see why he couldn't stay here. A little while anyway."

"Sure would appreciate it. What's the fee I wonder?"

"For you? Hundred dollars ought to do it."

Lee reached for his wallet.

"But you got to be gone by six o'clock."

"I can do that."

"Say, is that your car out there?" He laughed.

"Maybe he'd like to play checkers."

"No, not really. No, I . . ." He stopped. There was a calendar with the picture of a girl on it, one of the nudest such girls he had recently seen. Another woman was in the kitchen that lay over against this room, its door wide open.

"Looks like you need some coffee," she said in a friendly voice.

"No, not actually, thanks anyway. No, I just need to get to bed. Half a cup might be good."

"Needs to get to bed," the first man noted. "Wouldn't think he'd need a revolver for that."

"You going to show him that room, or not?

He was led by a third man to the west wing and thence to room number 6, a barren cell with an air mattress and a pile of dubious underwear in the northeast corner. Required to pay in advance, Lee drew off into the bathroom and after pulling his watch out by the chain and probing to the bottom of the pocket, drew out one hundred dollars precisely in the form of twenty-dollar bills. The man expected a tip, however.

Left alone, Lee sat on the toilet, the sole place for taking the weight off his feet. He could hear music from another of the rooms, a noise from out of Africa just now coming to western ears. An undiscoverable cicada had taken a position somewhere. Apart from his unremitting folly, he could just as easily have been at home with his wife, hidden among books, the refrigerator full of good things. Twenty minutes he sat in that place, his mind reviewing this and other mistakes, his dead relatives, lost acres, books that he had read.

Five

In fact, he passed yet another five minutes in that location and then arose and crept to his car and drove back stealthily to Bertram's place. The girl was still there, her mouth just as fully open as before.

"Hi!" he said in a friendly tone. "Thought I'd give you another chance!"

"What, they give you room 6?"

"Yes, they did."

"You got $72.50?"

"Plus tax? Yes, I do."

He paid, extracting the bills one by one from, first, his watch pocket and secondly his vest. The girl was following a love story on television in which the male, abnormally handsome, was gazing deeply into the eyes of an exquisite-looking girl with prominent breasts. The clerk meantime was permitting her ice cream to drip into her lap. Running his mind backwards, Lee envisioned her at nineteen, possibly a pretty thing at that time.

He repaired to his room, opened the door, and then leapt inside in order to foil anyone who might have schemed to pounce on him and take his things. It was a mediocre place; he'd seen better, and just two minutes previously he'd seen worse. As for the bed, he'd never seen worse than this, a thing of irregular shape that proved to have been short-sheeted once he gathered his nerve and drew down the covers. Or cover rather. Using his right foot, he turned the television to the wall and then went and tested the toilet. The tub was immaculate but not so the water itself, which bore a resemblance to glycerin until he deduced finally how to open the drain. He explored the closet, too, coming up with an unclean pair of panty hose and a wad of cellophane.

In old days, Lee had generally been able to preselect in his dream for the night—a blizzard in French Canada in 1730 or thereabouts with red Indians all about. Or, he might see himself pouring over dimly-lit maps in the captain's quarters of a frigate under sail in the South Pacific. But that he should persist in this sort of self-deception at the age of seventy-eight . . . He blushed, laughed, smote himself on the forehead, and got into bed.

He dreamt it was a cold winter's night in French Canada in 1730 or thereabouts. A few moments of this and he began to veer over into memories of his extinct ancestors—farmers and whatnot, mail carriers, almoners, and the like. In recent decades he had come to believe that immortal life was no more implausible than the findings of modern physics, and that indeed the dead might be with us still, albeit in some other room in the cell block of existence. In a case like that, the living and the extinct might be seen as allotropes of one another, and nothing to keep them apart save a very thin and indeed rather fragile sheet of water-colored *Time*.

That torn page found in the top drawer of his bedside table? It seemed to be an advertisement for a pair of inexpensive shoes available through the mail. The verso, on the other hand, or other side rather, gave just one part of a paragraph of a poorly-written adventure story dealing with alligators. Half asleep and the rest of him awake, he tried to finish the story in his imagination, but then shortly reverted to the French Canadian situation of 1731. It was then he heard a commotion.

In the event, it was a great black automobile lodged in the earth. He watched cynically for a moment—the driver was a woman—but then slowly and not without exasperation got into his suit and tie. He knew these people; years might go by, and still they'd be rocking back and forth in the tenuous topsoil (mixed with sand) that overspread these central counties. Knowing what awaited him, he hated to get into his burnished shoes.

The woman was rich—he saw that right away from the confusion on her face. She wasn't accustomed to these proceedings, nightmarish incidents that seemed to her a violation of the nature of things. Nevertheless, even so, he went around to the driver's window and put on an avuncular smile that couldn't fail to put her partly to rest.

"Ma'm?" ("Ma'm"? He was by much the older of the two.) "Do you need help?"

She spoke, but owing to the window no one could hear. They looked at each other.

"Could I help?"

"Oh, God." (It was one of those windows that move up and down under hydrostatic pressure.) "I'm stuck!"

"Yes."

"And I can't get out!"

"I divined as much. Are you staying here at this motel?"

"Lord no. Here? No, I was just over at Maude's and Fred's when *this* happened. Oh God, I don't even know what part of town this is!"

"Follows. I suppose I could pull you out with . . ."

"Oh, would you?"

". . . my worn-out Fraser."

"Oh, would you? I'll pay you."

"Pay me?" He had to laugh. "Madam, I'm seventy-eight years old; what does money have to do with me? How much are we talking about exactly?"

"You speak so well. But why are you staying *here*?"

"Research."

"Oh."

Therefore, he did link up his old car with her new one and after a dramatic struggle staged for her benefit alone, did manage to extract the vehicle.

"This has never happened to me before, *never*!"

"Anything can happen these days. Never forget that."

"And you've just got to let me pay you."

"It's my bumper don't you see. Twisted like that." (It *was* twisted.) "Very hard to find a replacement these days. Impossible actually."

"Oh, I *am* so sorry. So very, very sorry."

"I was going to sell it into the antique market. But they won't buy it now, that's for sure."

Her face was a mask of anguish. Coming nearer, he could see where the effects of her make-up had succeeded and where they had failed.

"Well maybe I could just buy *the whole car*. Now how would that be?"

"Not fair. Not fair to you, ma'm."

"I tell you what, why don't you just let me decide what's fair. All right?"

Lee grinned appealingly. "All right. I reckon."

They drove through a Chinese district with the usual lanterns and thence to a turquoise mansion in the good part of town. It was here, presumably, that her money was kept. He rushed to her side of the car and, stepping back, opened wide the door. He estimated her as at about fifty years in age, depending upon the light.

The place must have had twenty rooms, including a library in which the tomes, leather bound, most of them, ran from floor to ceiling in cherry wood shelving edged with brass. Lee came and pressed his nose against the glass.

"Egad," as he expressed it. "Just look at that!"

"Yes. And it cost a fortune I want you to know. Paying those people to pick them out and set them up like that. Coffee?"

She exunted to the kitchen and muttered a word or two to a displeased-looking factotum, a black woman with massy buttocks of the sub-Saharan kind. It was by now almost two o'clock in the morning and Leland had by no means taken all the sleep he needed. "I had intended," he said, speaking to himself alone, "to make a last trip to the Gulf of Mexico. And is *this* the Gulf of Mexico?" (He waved his arm about, pointing to the larder and the cabinets, the copper cookware and aluminum stove with the six eyes on it.) "It is not."

He kept on talking, which is to say until the black woman turned and gave him a frightened expression. He laughed. "No, no, I'm not *completely* insane. Not yet."

"Not?"

"Too much reading, that's all. By the way, where did your . . ." He had started to say "mistress," as in "where did your mistress go? He actually did say: "what happened to your associate?"

The woman never answered. Nor had Leland yet been given coffee or anything else. The price of his ancient automobile was rising by the minute. He saw, he thought, a tinted jar full of pickled peaches, but immediately spat out a tiny sample of the stuff when he found the contents were but an artifice of some kind. They did look like peaches, he admitted that. Far away, he could hear the two women speaking in low tones, and further still, the sound of a television set. Beyond that, the noise was of "music," the sound of a turpitudinous youth with an androgynous voice. Other sounds came from far and near.

"Pardon me," said Lee loudly. "I'm still here right where you left me, but I don't know whether . . ." His voice petered out. The next room had an aquarium full of abnormal-looking fish in all sorts of unlike sizes. Next to that, a grandfather clock with a harvest scene engraved on the face. He penetrated into a child's bedroom where the child herself lay with her toe in her mouth and on her face a blasé expression that seemed to say she had seen quite enough of life already. His best project was to return at once to the kitchen; instead, he climbed to the second-story balcony and set about examining the advanced art works arrayed along the wall. Soon, he was engrossed in a tableau of two dots set in the upper left corner of one of the canvases. That was when the woman entered and then stepped back when she saw him positioned there.

"Oh!"

Lee also stepped back. They looked at one another until Lee could choose one of his standard smiles and put it on.

"Quite a fine collection you have here!"

The woman still needed some time.

"Yes. You have good taste," she said. "We're so proud of this one especially."

"Well, I can see why. Three dots!"

"And triangle. No, this was done by one of our local boys."

"Whew." He turned to the negress with the coffee. She was a weary-looking quantity carrying far too much weight both fore and aft. She might or might not be pregnant in both places. Lee sipped at the coffee, no doubt a foreign import, and turned it back to the servant. "More sugar please."

They gathered in the great room, the woman, her husband, and the ageing Lee. Having acclimated to each other, Leland learned everything he wanted to know about the family, namely that the woman was her husband's brother's former wife's cousin, now involved in an open marriage with the man sitting across from Leland. Conducting simultaneously a lesbian affair with her second-youngest son's tennis coach, she was acting as councilor to the Associate Head, recently acquitted, of the Equalities Council.

"More coffee?"

"Please."

"I was telling my husband—that's him over there—that you saved my skin tonight!"

Lee looked at her skin. "Bad neighborhood," he admitted.

"And you just about *ruined* that darling little car." She turned to the man sitting in half-light at about thirty-five feet from Lee. "And we *have* to do something about that. Right?"

"It's three o'clock in the goddamn morning!"

Even now, the coffee was not as sweet as it ought to have been. Lee sent her back, this time pointing into his palm for the amount of sweetening he required. Meantime, a dog had entered the salon, a runty creature with a substance leaking from her even-numbered nipples. Moving gingerly, Lee was able to situate his groin out of the animal's reach. This room also had paintings in it, not excluding a noble-looking etching of Leon Trotsky against luminescent clouds. Realizing finally how advanced these people were, Lee commenced to speak of Fraser cars and associated costs.

"It wouldn't be worth so much if it weren't so *old* you understand. An *incunabulum*, I like to call it."

They smiled, neither of them supplied with the least idea of what he was talking about. Lee went on:

"Last I checked, Aldus was getting a good seventeen thousand for his *Sophocles*."

"Oh, dear."

"And that's not even fifteenth-century!"

He accepted the coffee but hadn't time to test it before the maid had run away.

"It's nothing in this world but a goddamn bumper! Besides, I want to see it!" the husband put in.

"And my wife hasn't really been well these last few years," Lee admitted. "And me, look at me."

"You don't look so bad. Except for that monkey suit you're wearing. Okay, how about a thousand dollars? That ought to cover the goddamn bumper *and* leave enough for a good cup of coffee!"

"A *good* cup? That would be wonderful."

"Oh, Lester. We can do better than that."

"Much better. Anyway, that bumper is well-nigh irreplaceable. After all, it's not as if one wanted just to buy a pound of beans is it? Fungible things available anywhere?"

"Pound of beans," the man said softly. "All right, I'll make it two thousand. But I get to keep the car!"

"Ah. And how, pray, will I get home again?"

"He *has* to get home, Lester."

So went the negotiation, continuing until 3:47 when the man wrote out a check for six-and-one-half thousand American dollars and then accompanied Lee to the door and helped him forcibly into his automobile. He had expected, had expected Lee, bright lights and movie theatres, taverns, "vibrant" peoples, and early morning bakeries with ethereal scents; in fact, the city was as moribund at this hour as since the previous afternoon. It had, after all, just 2,300 persons, too small for an active performance market but too large for Lee.

Six

Returned to his ruined car, Lee tipped the cab driver with an amount greater than the fare and then hurriedly moved the Fraser to a cluttered area not worth the effort to describe it. It was almost 4:20 in the morning, a chill was up, and the clouds overhead had coalesced to an extraordinary density. Many hours had gone past since he had deserted his hillside home, and yet he was hardly any nearer to the Gulf than if he had been traveling in reverse.

His motel room, seemingly, was as he had left it, the pillow and other things crumpled in the same way and the little tell-tale cipher (about the size of a dust mite) had either been left alone or else put back in place by someone with special training. Going to the mirror, he verified the image there and then turned on the television in the hope that the static would carry him off to sleep again. Soon enough, he would have perfect silence everywhere he went. That was when he experienced something he had experienced before—a smell of dumplings and boiled chicken insinuating into his cell.

Apart from two cigarettes and three cups of Near Eastern coffee, he had consumed almost nothing since setting out. Most reluctantly, he rose from his canted bed and began going through his wardrobe. He had rather perish than wear the same suit for more than ten connected hours; furthermore, his haircut was out of sync. All his life, he had been possessed of grey sunken cheeks and no matter how vehemently he slapped himself, never had he been able to bring much color to that region. Finally, his money, hundreds of dollars dispersed on his person, and in his vest a chit worth $6,500.

Mind functioning at high speed, he sauntered for some hundred rods in the wrong direction before correcting his trajectory and aiming for a desolate-looking restaurant with the neon likeness of a rooster vaunting on the roof. Unless those be last year's decorations, the people had already decorated the place for Christmas, a brilliant scene featuring the Easter Bunny with a basket of colored eggs. Lee pulled open the door—it was heavy—leapt inside, and then stood for a moment apprising himself of the riff-raff sitting as far apart from each other as possible. He had seen some morose establishments in his day, but none moroser than this. It lightened his spirits and pointed him to an empty booth near the rear.

He saw this: an exhausted accordion player nodding off to sleep, a party of two women speaking simultaneously into one another's ear, a workman of some type with a metal box held between his feet, and finally a loathsome youth wearing a sneer. But mostly Lee's attention was for the waitresses, a sad profession that always brought the nobler part of him to the surface and inspired his largest tips. Given a menu, Lee opened it like a museum-quality art book and immediately sought about for the photograph of chicken and dumplings that he had been so certain would be there. He did find the picture of a wedge of pie with ice cream on top and, wasting no further time, summoned the nearest waitress and pointed to it.

"And coffee," he cited, relocating his revolver. "Domestic."

He got his ice cream but the pie never came. Relying on his patience, he then called the tinier of the waitresses and asked again for a slice of domestic pie. She wrote it down.

"So, you like it here then, do you? Being a waitress? My first wife, she used to work in a place almost as wretched as this. Before she took her Ph.D."

"We have apple pie."

"And what's the story over there with that other waitress? Looking kind of peaked wouldn't you say?"

"Her mother isn't doing well at all."

"Oh? Well at her age, her mother's age I mean, she doesn't really have much responsibility for her mother anymore. Right?"

"They're real close."

"Ah, over*weaning* types!" he said, snorting at what really was one of his best witticisms in days.

"Yes, sir."

"Okay, apple will be fine. Cinnamon on it."

He got his cinnamon and got his pie. Got his coffee,

too, and never mind that it had a sediment in it. Geared up for the main course, he asked for three several pieces of boiled chicken, two of them breasts. The dumplings were good and had a white cream on them that invested the biscuit as well. Turning slantwise (so as not to disgust the others), he consumed this material in his special way.

There was a portrait on the wall of a famous president and next to that, the actual card of a bingo victory. There followed the photo of a man showing off an exceptional catfish, his son gazing up rapturously at what was unquestionably his father. But that was years ago and no doubt they despised each other now. Just then, the smaller waitress cut across his view, giving proof that she had no figure whatsoever. This led him on to a consideration of the horrible fate that lies in wait for the generality of women and girls. Himself, Lee resembled a weasel and worse, none of it interfering with his career as it had worked itself out over time. Ah, but let a woman's nose be a few inches too long or short, her mammae out of kilter, and she could expect to live alone. He sorrowed for them, a species that must worry about appearances as soon as probated from the womb. Thinking these and related thoughts, he called upon the primary waitress, saying:

"It's terrible, about your mother. Is she getting good care? I have six thousand dollars."

"Fair to middling. But she just won't eat nothing."

Lee glanced at his own plate, where much of the food remained. "Get her a private nurse! Shit, I'll take care of that part."

"No, sir. She don't want nobody else."

"Lord, Lord, Lord. Imagine you had grown up to look like . . ." (He mentioned here the name of a certain famous actress.) "Why Lord, you'd have *all sorts* of lovers and husbands to help you out!"

"I expect so, yes, sir. More coffee?"

It was too late. She must have been more than forty

years in age and already had turned primarily to fat. She didn't care. And then, too, Lee could discern how she had rolled her hose up just over her knees and no further. Five o'clock in the morning, he wanted to cry.

He moved back slowly to his own domicile, cutting through a long line of Asian immigrants moving forward by lantern light. Mississippi was full. In his room, the static had somewhat improved, and he was able to fall off into a mediocre grade of sleep that compared to just about a "five," or "six" on his personal ten-scale. He was a man who could travel three hours for each of sleep, and stalk through southern towns on 400 calories or less. Therefore, he was a gaunt person with a mind that was as clear and as clean as an average eighteen-year-old's who just happened to be a genius. Dangerous, too, since he had given up on fear and was as likely as not to do things to people.

He woke again. Dismayed by the sun, he shut the curtain and after some trouble managed to hang the spare blanket in such a way as to reduce the light, an insidious substance, yellow and grainy, titrating into the room. There was no question but that he had neighbors on the other side of the wall, and no question but that the man of the family was shaving, judging from his little electrical appliance that gave off a bee-like noise. Was it possible that Lee would get no further sleep that night? And of course there were the usual heavy-duty trucks far and near, all of them struggling simultaneously to get into second gear.

"Goddamn it!" he confided. No use trying to recollect his dreams for the night, save that one of them, the worst, had him face to face with a satanic individual whose will power was greater even than Lee's. Suddenly he rose up (Lee) and began to go through his clothes, finding all his funds intact. He'd of given a large sum just now for a cup of home-brewed coffee, not to mention a fresh package of

Kentucky cigarettes and a late-breaking copy of his habitual newspaper. Instead, altogether exhausted, he got into his uniform and one shoe and then, seeing that the job was almost done, rested for a while in the aftermath of his achievement.

His favorite newspaper was produced in Arizona, and he was very seldom able to put his hands on a copy. True, there was a library in Montgomery with a valuable array of dailies from different parts of the country. More than that, the librarian there was a sympathetic sort of person who allowed him to smoke. He realized he was digressing just now.

He departed the room, returned for a second piss, and then aimed himself, not toward his restaurant of the night before, but toward some other place. Here the waitress did have hips, also a face that was about as ruthless as any he had seen prior to that time. He succeeded in placing himself at the further end of the narrow room where the support staff seemed more or less normal to him. This waitress also at first seemed normal, though it nonplussed him somewhat when she took down his order by tape recorder.

". . . and three strips of bacon," he finished up.

"Oh, my," she responded. "Cholesterol!"

Lee waved her off. With nothing to do, no books or newspapers at hand, he gathered up the salt and pepper shakers and examined the contents. A far more complicated molecule, that of pepper as compared to salt. Suddenly he jumped back, startled to see that the booth was supplied with a cut-glass pink-hued saucer holding what looked like either Valium or Viagra tablets.

Three times he changed tables in an ongoing effort to keep out of the sun, finally coming upon a place whence he could monitor the pedestrians wending crooked paths to their respective office buildings. Lee could not but smile. Through the unclean glass he exchanged glances with a middle-aged woman who had far preferred to be done with progress and allowed to stay at home on the farm. Next, he saw a man whom he didn't care for at all, equipped as he was with a face that was both weak and yet phlegmatic all at the same time. They looked at each other. It was a nation of insurance salesmen, improvement committees, roofing contractors, dieticians, and real estate people, all standing on the shoulders of tobacco farmers and Indian killers.

He gulped down his bacon and sausages and drained his coffee to the lees. Our man was seventy-eight years old but didn't feel a day older than seventy-six. Rising and yawning and lifting out his wallet, he left money enough to cover the invoice together with a generous bonus for the woman who had fetched his provender. In any case, the place was getting rather too crowded for his taste, and he was able to identify at least two other parties unacceptable to him owing to their behavior and personal properties in general.

The day was chill, clouds rolling in. And was it chill and were it cloudy over his homestead in old Crenshaw County? He knew only that he remained very far from the Gulf of Mexico, and prime fishing season must soon be over.

He repaired to his hotel, gathered his tackle and other belongings, and then went to confront the woman at the desk, a superannuated hag who stirred up comradely feelings in a man who also was ageing very rapidly. First, he allowed her to see how much money he had and then, secondly, managed to reposition his revolver without perturbing her overmuch. She was a good old egg, as they say, and laughed along with him.

"I hope you enjoyed your stay with us," she offered with seeming sincerity.

"Of course. Except for that character next door who

was shaving at 5:35 in the morning."

"Yes, that's where we live, Billy and me."

"And the sun."

"Well, we can't do much about that now, can we?"

She laughed merrily, but Lee did not. A congress of young Carlists and some four or five neo-Pythagoreans, as Leland viewed them, had assembled in the lobby where they were insulting one another in the received manner. Lee noted the pigtails and earrings and odd-looking glasses. One of the theorists held a contraption to his ear while with the other hand he went on leisurely scratching his gonads.

"Ignore them," Lee advised. "They're just trying to inflame the bourgeoisie."

"Bourg . . . ?"

"Philistines, madam. But I had far lief entrust myself to *them* than . . ." (He motioned toward the scum.) ". . . scum."

His lovely old car was where he had left it, a crowded place still not worth describing. Using his strength, he easily repaired the rear fender, causing it to be largely straight again. How he loved it, to get behind the wheel of this sturdy "capsule," as he thought of it, that fenced him off from the outside world and its bad music. This time, he inserted his .357 into the holster affixed to the door and after taking the two indigestion tablets contributed free of charge by the café, counted up to three and started up the engine. Right away he saw that he would be driving *into* the sun, an awful omen that sent him back to his map and compass. He might be able to take another road entirely and still get himself to the Gulf in time for the annual run of redfish and shrimp.

Seven

But had not gone six miles before he began nodding off

to sleep. It was the sun, you realize, the most blatant thing in the sky, and never would he understand how civilized people could manage to remain awake while *that* was shining. Accordingly, he left the highway at his first good opportunity and proceeded along a gravel road that pointed generally toward Florida, he believed. He checked his watch, finding that the creature's little black arm pointed to just past seven in the morning. Here, with the path narrowing in on him, he opted to halt and smoke and even perchance to abandon the car and sleep among the trees, a denouement he had recently wished for.

It was not a comfortable arrangement, and instead of falling off to sleep, he began to study the encompassing woods through his somewhat cracked and cloudy (cloudy because of age and cracked because of mishaps) spectacles. He saw, he thought, a pinecone falling to earth, a piece of random litter, a persimmon tree devoid of fruits. No sound reached him in that milieu, not even that of distant trucks cycling through their gears. But for a high-volt tower about a mile away, he might almost be back in seventeenth-century times with red Indians all about. He searched for and quickly found his .357 revolver, his ammunition, and seven-inch ice pick. Especially his revolver, a silver instrument made of electrum which he clasped to his chest. He could fall off to sleep immediately now, but first he must settle upon a dream.

He dreamt that his wife and he were domiciled in a tiny fortress in the French-Canadian wilderness with snow and ice all about. It was so cold in those days, so very so, they had to clasp one another tightly in their narrow bed. Next, he dreamt that he was dreaming, dreaming in the arms of that woman who had been designated for him from the beginning and whose form was so perfectly congruent with his own. For they were lying under a woolen blanket, and on top of that an aged but devoted dog.

His third dream had to do with one of the northeastern

Alabama volcanoes that had exploded while he was sleeping. He could run as fast as anyone (anyone his age) but could *not* realistically expect to escape the lava. (His second dream had been a mere fragment only, too inconsequential to mention.)

Finally, he put these worries off to one side and began to sleep in real earnest. His brain, never completely dormant, dwelt on a variety of things. Checking his watch, he verified that it was just before 2:00 and then, next, that it had turned to late afternoon. Pleased with himself, he got out of his pajamas, folded his blankets, and wormed his way, not without difficulty, into his second-best suit, a dark grey double-breasted business that let him look his age. True, he did need a haircut and true, too, that he had mislaid his initialed handkerchief. He furthermore needed to shave, but at the same time needed to conserve his razors.

Taking his gun with him, he wandered deeper into the trees and eliminated. He had seen no animals or insects of any kind, and yet the forest continued to produce a stridulating sound that seemed to arise from the earth itself. Here, the flora was the color of squash and each red leaf a ticket to paradise. He tried to close his eyes but right away began teetering back and forth in the way that betokened his old age. Pellucid and mellow, pied, dappled, and mottled, the meadow was accentuated with orchards of lopsided plums. This much he knew for a certainty, that *landscape*, properly speaking, was just one more effort in a long string of them to grant Leland an unearned preview of the hereafter world.

He must have spent half an hour in that "sylvan interlude," as later described, before then coming out into the open just as a low-orbiting drone passed overhead. Immediately, he put on a wholesome smile and opened both fists to prove he wasn't carrying anything.

He drove then for perhaps eleven miles before the

highway veered off in an eastwardly direction. It didn't bother him; the car was full of gasoline, and he still remained within a forty-mile perimeter of his wife and acres, his canned fruits and vegetables, his book hoard and carpentry tools. He had weapons, too, and seven suits with well-matched ties. Was this a good time to die, dying at fifty-three miles an hour? Would a speed like that not perhaps give him a flying start to the next phase in his ten-thousand-year biography? Thinking of it, he turned on the radio and nudged the dial back to that obsolete channel that just now was playing one of his all-time favorite songs.

The next hour passed more or less normally, nothing unusual coming his way. He passed a car, the first time he had managed to do so since starting out. The agriculture in these parts was mostly of corn and soybeans with an occasional dairy added in for good measure. Of course, modern people don't care greatly for such observations, though they be standing unawares on the shoulders of corn and beans and, yes, weathered old men in overalls with tobacco stains running down their chins. Just then, a little yellow car of foreign origin ran past, inside it some four or five grinning youths of the arts and humanities type.

He couldn't catch them, and after a short time he slowed and put away his Smith & Wesson. Where once there had been soybeans, he now noted the beginning of a shopping center and two square miles of parking space. He recalled to mind an old-fashioned grist mill modified now into a sun-tan salon. His intention was to hurry on past this mess and get himself back into open countryside again; instead, that was when he had to stop for a funeral cortège turning across in front of him.

A male had died, a white one as he was able to determine from the size of the hearse. Bending forward, Lee tried to read the faces in the first cars, finding one or two that might be sincere. And he, Lee, how many such faces would attend *his* final rites, or listen with attention to Mahler's *Abschied,* to be performed immediately thereupon. Not one, he had to admit.

He didn't care, not so long as they lowered him quickly and packed the earth up to a decent height. Not so long as his stone bore the right quotation from Simonides and he be insulated all around with Passion Flowers in his box. Or so long as the authorities buried with him the seventeen books listed in his will, he didn't care.

Thus Lee, weeping as he waited with deteriorating patience for the long line of cars to turn off and proceed slowly to the visible little graveyard situated at no great distance from the highway. Using his binoculars, Lee then spotted an above-ground vault with sculptures on it, a thing more appropriate for himself than for the wretched little businessman and/or public official currently quarantined inside it. It aggravated him, causing him to smoke and hum and then, his patience at an end, caused him *to enter the cortège himself* and follow where it went.

It went less than a hundred rods before steering off into a parking area, the people getting slowly out of their cars and trundling sadly up the hill. Lee was just as well-dressed as any of them, and his demeanor at least as grave. He stepped past a Confederate inhumation where an unidentified soldier—Lee had begun to weep again—lay among his weapons. Stay here long enough and see the fusilier rise up in tremendous wrath and, turning toward the North, march with giant steps in that direction—this is what Lee wanted.

Instead he moved to join the crowd of some two-dozen gathered about the burial site. He insisted upon viewing the casket, forcing him to squeeze forward through the mourners. It was a luxurious affair, the man's coffin, and had a golden filigree that ran around the lid. He assumed, Lee, that the interior was just as fine and provided the man a wonderful resting place along with his wedding ring and the half-dozen laminated newspaper clippings that mentioned family members. He assumed other things, namely that the mortician had done good work, pretty good, owing to his long-time acquaintanceship with the deceased. Getting into the mood of it, Lee was easily able to pick out the widow from among the women, a fifty-year old, he believed, who had collapsed in such a way that her legs were actually dangling in the pit. He rushed to help her but was forestalled by two other Southern men who lifted her up and braced her in a standing position.

The remainder of the ceremony took place over a period of about twenty minutes during which time the pastor read some of Leland's pet phrases from Ecclesiastes. Came now the descent of the casket into the red clay earth. Lee pressed nearer, appalled at the seepage of water that already had arisen an inch or two above the bottom of the vault. Soon, the dead man would be floating in the stuff, and never mind the needlework and unguents so carefully lavished on him.

"Ghastly business!" he said, causing the widow and several others to glance up at him. "And yet it wasn't so long ago that he was a young man, full of good looks and all kinds of energy. Striding through the fields!"

But he had been wrong to imagine his words would appease the woman. Bitter looks were cast in his direction. That was when he discerned a bright red worm that had glued itself to the wall of the casket. Lee pointed at the thing, but then changed his mind and scratched his nose instead.

"Shoot," he said, "these modern caskets can remain waterproof for *years*, they claim." And then: "Time to cover him up I guess."

He watched respectfully as three several men, also about fifty years in individual age, came out with an equal number of new-looking shovels and began, tenuously at first, to toss wet clay down upon the mahogany cover. Pushing his mind forward, he tried to summon up in imagination the response of the geneticists of the future, educated men who would know how to bring Southerners back to life again. With that in mind, he began to edge his way to the widow where she lay face down, peeping into the grave. Already some of the less committed people had begun to sidle toward their cars, leaving the process in stronger hands.

"Shoot," said Lee. "Twenty years, thirty at most, they'll be able to do all sorts of things with dead bodies. For example, who would ever have thought that we'd have ballpoint pens and washing machines?"

"That's right." (This from a skewbald hillbilly with a shriveled pate, also about fifty in age.) "We'd be in big trouble without pens and things. Why, I can remember when . . ."

Lee held up his hand to stop him. "Please. I was speaking of *genetics*, actually. The findings of modern chemistry, and so forth."

"Oh. You the fellow in that investment club? He wanted me to join, too, but I never got around to it."

"Please."

"Okay. We can talk about it at the commemoration."

Lee waited for his disappearance and then returned to the widow. She was supported by two men and their accomplices, all of them intimidated by Lee and all of them wishing to be elsewhere.

"Parallel universes, ma'am. Perhaps it will be as if one simply steps into another room, *graduating*, if you will, into a higher realm."

"I'm not so sure about that."

Lee turned upon the fellow, but then immediately relented and put on a cordial face.

"No, of course not. After all, how could a person like yourself, how could you possibly have any connection with *transcendent* values, hmm? No, no, I'm not saying it's *your* fault. Always remember that."

He agreed to do so and then, blushing, turned and remanded himself to his aged pick-up with the feed bags in it. The residual crowd, some eight or nine persons all told, had begun to chaperon the widow back to the Limousine—it surely wasn't hers—in which she had come. At first, Lee started to take a seat in the front, and did. It was a little past five o'clock in the day, and he was actually moving further from, as opposed to nearer to, the Gulf of Mexico.

It was a mediocre landscape, the one they were passing by on both sides. He spied a barn that he had spied before, a cavernous structure with space enough inside for two of every creature on earth. Saw a forlorn man carrying a bucket somewhere, a survivor of the agrarian age. More significantly still, they passed a tumbled-down antebellum neo-classical mansion that had been handed over, it seemed, to black people with drug addictions. He tried, vainly, to have the widow look at the scene.

"Fine man, your husband," he conceded. "But you're not so old that you couldn't still . . ."

Came then a voice from the back seat: "Tell you what, why don't you just leave her alone? And by the way, while we're on the subject, I'm still not so sure we even know who you are!"

Lee reacted: "So this is your gratitude then? No good deed goes unpunished, right?"

"Naw, he's part of that stocks and bonds mess Frank got mixed up in."

"Those weren't stocks. Those were *futures* for Christ's sakes."

"Damned near ruined him, whatever they was."

"Don't matter. He's ruined now anyway."

They snickered, one of them. Lee took account of the fact that they had left the highway and were riding, none too smoothly, toward an unremarkable house worth perhaps 30–35 thousand dollars exclusive of the grounds. Lee was a little surprised that so many chickens had been left alive, a populous herd that would have to be fed through the winter months and likely as not would turn out even thinner than they currently were. On the other hand, he was assuaged by the fields, the cubes of hay, and a leaning silo that harkened back to certain descriptions preserved in English literature.

There was a pot of beans and syrup left on the porch. This, too, appealed to Lee, who respected the old-time custom of soothing the bereaved with hot food and cornbread, biscuits and honey, and the like. Lifting the container with care, he moved it to the kitchen where an old-time negro stood waiting for it.

"Beans!" said Lee. "Hot ones."

"Well I declare."

"Go down real good in weather like this." And then in a much softer voice: "Your mistress has left the car and will be here very shortly."

They jumped to it, the negress taking down a heap of sky-blue dishes with sunflowers painted on them. He expected about fifteen persons, including children and the usual supernumeraries who—Lee knew them well—would have nothing to say. He expected three or four relatives as well, not to mention at least one real estate agent, a tax person and, no doubt, the family attorney.

"A real shame," someone attested, a fat man whose buttocks overlapped the chair. He delved into his pocket, took out a miniature knife, and began dithering with his nails. These preliminaries gave Lee the time to look into other rooms, but especially the parlor with its trivial little library of medical advice, a Bible, and four years' worth of high school yearbooks. He perceived a painting on the wall of Stonewall Jackson in full uniform, a calendar promoting a brand of snuff, and a wedding portrait of the deceased man and his wife. Lee wanted to cry. As for the mantel, it held a row of canned vegetables and a Chinese box acquired from the 1936 World's Fair. No one could open that box, and the people had given up trying—Lee was good at intuiting things of this kind.

The kitchen actually had a flour mill in the pantry, the first such one he had seen in years. There was an iron stove but, to be honest about it, didn't appear to have been employed for a very long time. There was a churn as well, this, too, now used more for decoration than anything else; he wanted to cry.

The chairs had all been taken, and for his own use, Lee had to fetch a children's stool from the east room. They were just beginning to talk about the dead man—stories, amusing incidents, proofs of his integrity—when the elder son drove up in a German car. Dressed better even than Lee, he rushed to his mother, squeezed her briefly, and then sought about for a sitting place. Lee judged him as of about thirty years in age, a city man with cufflinks and a notorious watch (notorious for cost) extruding from his sleeve. As for the daughter, she had wanted to come but had found herself "marooned," she wrote, somewhere on the Amalfi Coast. Lee, turning to face those two or three persons who had been following the farmer's career, said this:

"Thus falls a civilization that might almost have been like Greece."

Eight

And now when it grew dark, Lee rose up from the sofa and joined the woman and her brother at the table. He was a phthisic man, very tall and just as thin, who gave no great impression of anything. Lee looked at him. He felt terribly bad (the brother), but very clearly had no theories of what next needed to be done. As for the bowl of soup set in front of Lee, that had certainly been prepared by the woman and not at all by her brother.

"It's always the women," Lee started out, "who know what's essential and what not, and what needs to be done, yes?"

"True, very true," said the brother, awakening to the idea.

(They were seated at a circular table in the kitchen, a cozy location and particularly so for a person who had been fasting, more or less, for most of that day. Lee consumed the fluid part of the soup but saved the little bits of beef for very last. These he sprinkled lightly with pepper and then, rising and stretching, went and fetched the beans and molasses. It was all very good, and the strange shadows playing off the wall were also to his liking. He could hypothesize that these silhouettes were of Daphnis and Chloë running off hand-in-hand across the glebe. Or, a monstrous insect come to prey upon the widow. Finally, he pushed back and ignited the next-to-last of his foreign cigarettes, a powerful one that gave off little pops and other sounds as the individual shards caught fire.

"So!" Lee said, pulling himself back to the table. "Your husband had a position with the electric company?"

"Yes, sir." (Her mood was as gloomy as ever and he had to bend forward to pick up her voice.)

"And that will have been the major source of your income?"

"Yes, sir."

"And all this farming activity, the chickens and hay, don't tell me that was all for show?"

For the first time that day, the woman looked at him directly, saying:

"No, sir, we'd of been in big trouble if it was."

"Made over *two thousand dollars* just last year alone," the brother said, not without some trace of indignation in his tone. Suddenly, he got up, moved about the room, and then came back. "*Now* what are we going to do? Sir."

"I'm thinking about that." And then: "How'd he die exactly?"

"Transformer fell on him. But he went on living for near about two whole days."

"Ah. But he had insurance, right? With the electricity people?"

"Naw, they got him to sign some papers."

"But what about government benefits? And ethnicity—no points for that?"

"No, Lord. He were as white as me or you."

(They did have a monthly check of $126.43 from a trust fund established half a century prior to this, though Lee needed nearly an hour to learn about it.)

"You *cannot* live on hay and 126 a month; can't be done. No, you'll have to move in together, you two, and sell the farm. Agreed?"

Said the brother: "I don't know, just don't. I got two boys and a girl living over there with me already."

"Jove. And how old, pray, may these hatchlings be?"

"Steve, he's thirty-two. Don't know about Jeffrey. Now Rose, she's probably the oldest one."

"And you sir, how old were you when you left home?"

He calculated the years. "Believe I was 'bout fifteen in those days. Joined the Army. And boy howdy the food—that's what I remember about it. First time I ever had enough to eat."

"I was hoping to keep this house," his sister *inter alia* mentioned.

"Fifteen and thirty-two. Thus dies a society that might almost . . . Kick 'em out! Get rid of 'em for Christ's sakes! Get shut of 'em, and then you can take this good woman into your home!"

"Reckon I could. 'Course now my wife and her, they don't get along real good."

"Kick her out too! For Christ's sakes, what kind of man

are you after all?"

"I could." (His eyes sparkled.) "She'd sure put up one hell of a fight though." (He giggled.) "And the land is hers."

Lee moaned. Life was complicated and he too old to set things right.

"Kill her."

"Sir?"

"Okay, don't kill her. Hey, want me to do it? Naw, I'm just talking. Want me to?"

The clock showed eight o'clock, time for a certain Christian broadcast on the radio. Lee studied the pair as they settled respectively into a rocking chair and a love seat with gingham upholstery. No question but that the house and most of its things had been built by the family and its forebearers. His impulse was to go and hug the woman about her knees; instead, he took out his glasses and applied himself more seriously to the topic at hand. It was his fate, that he loved only obsolete people who were suffering from distress.

"You'll have to invest," he said.

"I told you," said the brother. "Told you he knows about stuff like that."

"Invest *entrepreneurially*."

"Whew! See what I mean?"

"We'll visit a broker tomorrow. Have to take risks of course. Bet the farm on it, for example."

"I was hoping to keep that." (Her eyes had run dry and looked like two red stones.) "Or the back forty anyway."

He awoke too early and failed to get back to sleep again. In general, he had a favorable opinion of roosters, but only when in a nostalgic frame of mind. The widow also was shaking him by the shoulder.

"Sir! Are you all right?"

"I was."

"It's five o'clock, and I seen you was still lying here!"

"Five! Got any coffee?"

"And we need to visit that fellow, like you said."

Her eyes remained like plums, and her hair was sticking out on one side. She had put on what probably was her best dress and wore a brooch with the likeness on it of a woman by Canova. Lee gazed at her steadily, summoning back to mind the events of the past forty hours. In his whole life, he had never been able to get him down to the Gulf of Mexico without vicissitudes of every kind.

With Lee at the wheel of the rented hearse, they drove westward for about two miles. He said nothing, Lee, when they encountered a fat man in a wrecker towing an early model Fraser in the opposite direction. He preferred, Leland Pefley, to focus upon the countryside, the advertisements, and the manifold little restaurants that specialized in barbecue and beer, smoke-filled places that he adored. He even focused upon the roadside litter and then, next, an escaped hog trundling forward at top speed in a fruitless effort to break free of civilization and its discontents. Next, he focused on other things, but especially a country girl, lithesome and in jeans, chasing after the animal with what appeared to be a butterfly net.

The broker dwelt in a modernistic structure made of glass. Lee's party exited the hearse, strode past a psychiatrist's office, a bondage studio, a public relations outlet in which two extraordinarily well-dressed men sat facing one another, and then, finally, a Hindu grocery with some peculiar-looking comestibles hanging from the ceiling. The following block had been settled mostly by Cambodians. Continuing on, he penetrated a Sudanese neighborhood where in old days had been a pastry shop.

They crossed at the intersection, parked, and entered a low-ceilinged room holding some dozen young men who together with a few random women in short skirts, all looked just alike. Lee's first impulse was to aim for the nearest fellow, a scrubbed type with one of those watches and oil in his hair. This was his second impulse as well, and it curtailed the time that would leave Lee's party just standing there. Intimidated by the scene, the widow's brother had already begun to retreat somewhat, which is to say until he backed into someone's desk, upsetting a little plastic cup of something.

"We're in the market for some *investments*," said Lee loudly, putting on a bored expression. "Capital gains, and that."

He was invited to sit, but the brother wasn't. As to the bereaved woman herself, she was dressed very respectably in the styles of circa 1920. The chair was comfortable, Lee's, and right away he lit up one of his blunts and began looking about for an ashtray and some coffee of his own. He was very well-dressed, and he knew it. Allowing the boy a few moments to gaze upon his tie, a broad one with a medieval theme, he lied:

"Yes, we've been meaning to come by and consult with you but, you know, with one thing and another . . . We buried her husband yesterday."

"Oh, I'm so sorry to hear it."

He was *not* sorry to hear it, and the whole world knew it. He had the magical ability to keep one eye on the tape while allowing the other to wander. Lee, putting himself in the way of that eye, spoke of investments, especially those that might be expected to make largest gains in the shortest possible time. The broker, who could not be more than twenty-eight, smiled in the patronizing way familiar to Lee from his time in New York City.

"Excuse me, 'sir,' but that's what everybody wants. Largest gains. Shortest time." He laughed, but then suddenly gave a little start when the first granules of Lee's tobacco began to crackle and pop.

"Long as I can keep my farm," the widow said.

"All right," Lee said, "very well, I can accept that. But what would *you* do, 'sir,' if *you* needed largest gains, shortest time."

The broker looked back steadily, his mind running freely over finance, the world, and associated things.

Well, if it was me, I believe I'd go into currency futures. Of course now I'm not recommending that in the present situation. Risky. *Very* risky. A person would have to be able to offset that with a steady income."

Lee raised his hand. "We have that. She gets a check *every single month* of the year. Like clockwork, one might say."

"I see! And this is a large amount, is it?"

The remaining brokers, never actually laughing out loud, were staring down at their desktops.

"One hundred and twenty-seven dollars," said the widow, trying to hide her arrogance.

"Hundred and twenty-seven?"

"And forty-three cents. But pssst, I don't even count that."

The boy's loose eye had left Lee and the woman and had joined with the other (other eye that is) in concentrating on the tape scrolling along the wall. Also glancing in that direction, Lee read that this year's Honduran endive crop was expected to disappoint. He looked for, but could not find, the widow's brother.

"I think we'll have some of those currency futures after all," Lee blurted out. "A few of 'em anyway."

"I don't advise it."

"Well of course not! You like to save those up for rich people, right?

Make sure they get in on the good stuff. No, I've read about this."

The broker demurred. It needed Lee to argue his position, and even then, he had to raise his voice to get what he wanted. Finally, at last, they agreed upon a hedge against the Ecuadorean *sucre*, a venture that could reap an economic "whirlwind," as Lee explained. Grudgingly, the broker took up an application form and began to question the woman about her full name, the size and location of her farm, and other desired information. It gave Lee the time he needed to exit the place and travel the few hundred rods to the dry cleaner where he planned to redeem his double-breasted brown suit with the lapels.

The place had four customers in it whom Lee encouraged to one side. As regards the woman behind the counter, Lee estimated that she had been standing in that spot for the past thirty years or more, her mind slowly decaying from the evaporations of dry-cleaning fluids. As always in such instances, he didn't know whether he more wanted to love her or take objective measure of her intellect. Her hair, which ought have been at least partly gray, was much too dark for the rest of her.

"I've come," he said, "to collect that brown suit with the wide lapels."

(There was music from the adjacent room, not the very worst that Lee had heard, though very near it.)

"Your name?"

He gave his name, a distasteful task for a person who gloried in obscurity. And if someday the authorities should come looking for him, might they not examine his dry-cleaning bills? It did please him that the woman had returned so quickly, an indication that her mind was not yet wholly gone. But displeased him that she had fetched the wrong suit, a snow-white ensemble that would have been too young for a seventeen-year-old.

"*Quoi*?" he said. "Ah no, my suit is brown, double-breasted, seven-inch lapels."

It distressed her. "Brown?"

"Yes, indeed. Lest you people have abstracted the color with your powerful fluids."

Again, she went back, a little bit of panic in her stride.

Through the open door, Lee could survey a whole world of highly unlike clothes, *women's* clothes, dangling from the hangers. "Ah," he said, speaking whimsically to himself alone, "if only these people could agree upon some permanent fashion, I do believe the national economy would revive." That was when he stepped back and smote himself almost violently on his forehead, saying "No. No, I expect they know what they're doing."

Said one of the women waiting in line:

"I was here long before he was!"

And then from someone else:

"You bet we know what we're doing! We do it for you!"

He conceded the point. And in any case, this last-mentioned person was rather a good-looking example with a satisfactory figure to go along with it. He bowed, very slightly, and saying nothing put on an ingratiating smile.

"Is this it? Sir?"

She had come back. Lee lifted the cellophane veil that protected the thing and tested the fabric between his thumb and finger. Far too coarse for any suit of his, the garment wasn't even brown.

"No, ma'm, this is a fifteen-dollar affair purchased from one of your local pawnshops. *My* suit costs 347 dollars, which is not even to mention the cents."

"Oh, dear. Let me check."

She went back, leaving Lee alone with three women, one of them a "six" on his evaluation scale. There was of course a calendar on the wall with the picture on it of a waterfall. Clearly, this was the aesthetic quotient of these people, an affinity for prettiness combined with ignorance. Lee gazed at the thing through narrowed eyes and then lit up one of longest of his cigarettes, a limp article bending toward the ground. Was she never coming back?

"Sir?"

Lee came awake.

"It looks like Junior Cobb has your suit. You must of given us the wrong name."

"Wrong name? Hardly. No, madam, I admitted what my name was when I entrusted it to you. 'Wrong name?' Ridiculous."

That was when a man, a large one in an apron, came to the counter and looked so coldly at Lee that Lee chose that same moment to look away.

"I can give you Junior's address," the woman persevered. Except for that, not a whole lot we can do."

He looked to heaven, Lee, trying manfully to stabilize himself against these concatenating haps. Worse still was the invoice for the suit, a hefty sum commensurate with a much larger project.

He left that establishment in a rage hidden by a smile. The last he wanted was to stir up animosity among the townsfolk who, one must suppose, were not significantly more peaceful than this sort of people the world over. He smiled at a woman in a peculiar hat and then, next, a policeman with a baton as large as a baseball hat. Smiled at the widow's brother emerging from the tavern, and smiled at the distinguished-looking Leland reflected in a window glass.

The widow was waiting in front of the building with a bundle of glossy brochures and a plastic medallion with the name of the brokerage on it. Leland, by no means accustomed to driving a hearse, tried to brake for her. The chill had put a stain on her cheeks, but her eyes were just as awful-looking as yesterday. Again, Lee stopped, this time to gather the woman's inebriated brother and cajole him into the back seat.

"Reckon I better put some hay out," the woman said. "Going to be cold."

"It *is* cold. But first I need to see a man about a suit."

Later on, he would remember the journey. It carried him to the intersection of state highway 127 and county road 43. There, turning at an angle, he lodged the hearse in the roadside ditch and only after many an attempt managed to get it out again.

"Now that really does surprise me," he said. "Not supposed to be like this."

"Sir?"

"Managing to get it out again."

Half a mile further, Lee tried to stop, failed, and then turned by necessity into a ten-acre junkyard containing at least a hundred and twenty wrecked cars all parked in the same direction. Thought he saw a Buick so much like his uncle's that he half expected to see the man himself. Saw all manner of Fords and Chevrolets, and a 1948 Fraser that seemed in good condition for a manufactured product nearly as old as himself.

One seldom saw such an item, and he couldn't be entirely sure of it until he left the hearse, strolled to the car, and examined its contents. Right away, he discovered a tattered 1864 first edition of Cockayne's *Leechdoms, Wortcunning, and Starcraft* in a seersucker binding, suggesting that the car was really his.

Joined by the widow and her brother, he went direct to the little wooden shack where the manager ought to be. In fact, the cell was empty. Lee examined the receipts and other papers that littered the desk, but neither there nor in the drawers did he come upon anything that pertained to his own personal automobile. "Hmm," he said. "Anyway, my guess is that a modern hearse is worth many times more than any old two-door sedan, what?"

It was a cloudy day, the trees bare, and the whole aspect of things was about as depressing as he had ever seen. Revivified by that, he moved the hearse into position and used it to nudge his own automobile out of formation and into a more or less open area. The widow herself he sent back to make a search for the key. Winter was coming in, no doubt about it, wherefore Lee's thoughts now began to turn to home, to a night alongside his wife, and a brief respite in company with some of Chatterton's more mature verse, as also perhaps that of a few others.

In truth, the town was even more depressing than that in consequence of which they encountered almost no traffic along the way. They passed a sheet-faced farmer in a pickup, a man with no expression in his face. Came next a stone monument in praise of the peanut, the county's chief source of trade. Here Lee halted for a moment, much interested in the graffiti that ran around the bottom quadrant of that peculiar thing.

"'Tommy loves Gwen,'" he read. And then, turning to the widow's brother, "Who was Gwen?"

"Her? Aw, she was just some little ole gal from around here. Dead now."

"Dead," said Lee to himself. "Dead and buried, but Tommy loves her still."

They crossed a bridge that spanned an extinct creek and then proceeded at reduced speed into the pith of the downtown metropolitan space. They passed a hardware store, a man out front signaling for customers to come inside. But all this passed away into nothingness when compared to the city drugstore, a brightly-lit-up enterprise with an old-fashioned soda fountain, now closed down. He'd have given his shoes just now for an old-fashioned ice cream soda with a spoon and two straws in it.

"Remember when we used to have soda fountains?" Lee asked the brother. "Ice cream sodas for fifteen cents?"

"No, sir; that was before my time I reckon."

"Yes? Well you'll soon be obsolete, too, and then we'll see how *you* like it!"

The woman's home was as they had left it, save that three further mourners had brought covered dishes and left them on the porch. In the hall, Lee noted two old suitcases and a dozen cardboard boxes, indications that the brother had come to stay. This man had a bit of an income surely, Lee believed, and that together with his sister's investments ought to see them through. Pleased with his work, Lee now drew off into the back room and stretched out on a dust-invested quilt inscribed with patchwork that told that good old story of the Flood.

Nine

It was full night when he awoke, an unasked-for blessing granted him by his own special star. Springing from bed, he ran to the kitchen for coffee but then hurried back just as speedily in order to pee. (Except for that, a man might go on sleeping for years.) The room had a calendar in it, a year out-of-date, with predictions in one margin and zodiacal symbols in the other. Putting on his glasses, Lee referred to his own birthday, a bale-boding day full of disappointment and old age. Impressed, he turned to the present time, a good date for hog slaughtering and candle making. How he loved it! These somber occupations, these pre-modern men and women who knew how to remain married, how to aim a rifle, how to manage negroes and produce autonomous sons.

The woman, who hadn't slept in seventy-two hours, was posted at the stove among her pots and kettles and a platter of waffles with little craters in them. Lee seated himself with delicacy, nodding to the brother who had tried without full success to wipe away the syrup about his chin. Lee could eat no fat, and the brother ate no lean, and between the both of them they licked their platters clean.

"Reckon I need to put out some hay," said the woman for the third time in almost that many days. Her brother raised his hand and, being recognized, said: "I'll do it in the morning Betty, him and me."

Meantime, the night owls had gathered just outside the window where in collaboration with the cicadas and the season's last crickets they produced the melancholiest noise imaginable. The walls were thin and imperfect, and from time to time Lee could see brief indications of silent lightning in the distance. The moon, too, insofar as he could detect it through the curtain, was "out of round" and seemed to be "dripping," as it were, as if composed of elements from the right-hand side of the periodic chart. Somewhere, a church was in session, and Leland could make out the sound of mournful singing from very far away. Soon they would be invaded with cruel winds from out of the north, a not unprecedented experience for that section of the country. Just then the woman shivered, inspiring the two men to mimic that contagious response. It *was* cold, and getting colder, and someday the whole world would be colder still. Lee arose and, taking the coffee with him, stepped into the back yard for kindling wood. The moon! Always susceptible to outright insanity, Lee believed he could make out a civilization in the lower left corner, an anthill sort of organization in which the inhabitants were always philosophizing, or painting pictures, or writing novels. He laughed then and slapped himself on the forehead, saving himself just in the nick of time from lunacy of the authentic kind.

They watched, brother and sister, as Leland piled the wood in the fireplace and tried to set it alight. Thus passed five, maybe ten minutes, until at last he produced a blaze sufficient to the need. Sooner or later, the flames would turn from orange to blue.

"Imagine," he said, speaking to the group at large, "imagine that log is *you*."

"No, Lee. I couldn't take much of that."

"Okay, imagine that blue part—see it?—imagine it's a celestial liqueur of some kind. Drink it down and you can see the future."

"Something wrong with you boy. How come you to talk like that?"

"He can't help it. Be nice," the woman said.

He said no more, Lee, at that time, not till he had turned his thoughts to more practical matters.

"All right, we're agreed on how we're to make a living, yes? We have the hay, we have our pension, we have those futures, and Wade here has a nephew who works in Birmingham."

"Yeah, and I got me some hogs, too. And around a hundert peach trees, near about."

"Still not enough. We're going to need at least another thousand. Each and every month."

"Can't get that kind of money Leeward, not less somebody goes out and gets her a *job*. And she don't want to."

They turned to the widow, who appeared not to have been listening. Except for her eyes and apathetic clothes, she was not a fully unattractive woman, not anyway above the waist. The two men studied her from their respective positions.

"She could of really been something. In her time."

"Still could! I mean if she wanted to."

"Women age more slowly, they say, in airconditioned office buildings."

"Yeah. And they got so many different kinds of jobs these days. Shit, Howard's wife makes near about *twenty thousand dollars* the year, sitting up there on the third floor."

"Twenty! Hear that, Betty?"

Her eyes were just about extinct by now, and yet she did try to see what they were talking about.

"Sir?"

"Twenty. However, we already have enough for the first year or so." (He reached for his wallet and after drawing out about 70% of his funds, spread them on the floor.) "And maybe I could teach French or something."

"*Vraiment*?"

"Certainly! Or raise bees. Of course, that's not like

twenty thousand a year. Not by a long shot!"

Night and its preliminaries had finished, bringing on a Devonian darkness in which even the owls were hushed. Putting on his best coat, Lee now began playing the part of a generic employer while the woman showed how she might approach him for a job.

"Never let anyone know that you're desperate for employment," he said. "Even if you are."

She nodded, the widow, and then knocked twice at the man's imaginary door.

"Come in."

"Sir," she said. "I can type, and . . ."

"No," Lee said. "That's not bad, but you need to be *far* more confident than that. Make them think that you plan to go out into society and make all sorts of money for the firm. That's what they like. And pull your skirt up a little higher."

Reluctantly, she did hoist her paisley skirt another half-inch or so. She had suffered from snake bite at some period, or perhaps had been pecked in that area by militant hens; in any case her upper calf region could by no means compare with those of urban girls, fifty years old or not.

"Jesus. Okay, explain how you've taken over the family operations and have all sorts of managerial experience—bookkeeping, etc. No wait, not bookkeeping; *accountancy* say. And public relations—they *really* like that."

She said it.

"Good. Now imagine Wade here doesn't have any magazine subscriptions, and you want him to buy, say, oh I don't know. *Yachting Times,* say."

"Sir, do you want to buy *Yachting Times*? It's real good."

"Alright! No, that's pretty damn good Betsy! What d'you think Wade?"

"Damn good. Sure enough."

"'Cause we're talking now about *commissions* Betty. You sell just one of these subscriptions and you get a percentage, don't you see. Sell a thousand and that's a . . .

"Thousand . . ."

". . . percentages!"

She smiled, the first such smile he had so far seen in her. Her eyes had taken on a grateful aspect.

They smoked. Or rather it was Lee who did the smoking, Wade who did the wine, and the widow who was talking to herself. An hour of this and Lee turned to the brother, saying "give us a story Wade."

"Well, seems like a bunch of those fellows had got it into their heads to go on down to Conecuh County 'cause of *free land* you understand. Anyhow, that's what the gov'mint said—free land. Well hell, they wern't no free land down there atall!"

The room fell silent. One single cricket remained on the outside windowsill, the last of its kind.

"My, God," Lee said finally. "Okay, tell us another one, okay?"

"Seems like old man Schrump got to shooting other people's cows. Got away with it, too, till they caught him."

"Good Lord. What happened then?"

"Don't rightly know."

"Well I reckon I'm going to retire to bed," the widow said, rising and retiring through the east side door. Lee retired in the opposite direction, leaving the brother to stare all night into a hoard of pulsing coals that looked like smirking faces. The hall was bare, save for one additional piece of luggage deposited there by the brother's wife. Lifting his candle to proper height, Lee attested to a series of five framed etchings delineating the stages of the French and Indian War. Suddenly he leapt back, discombobulated by the sudden entrance of a bright golden moth craving safety from the outside world.

His room was as before, except that someone had changed the linens. Working slowly—he knew he'd get no sleep in a night as perfect as this one—he took off his coat, his vest, and his shoes in that exact sequence. Next, he examined his buttons, finding a tiny length of loose thread of perhaps a quarter an inch. But his tie was as fresh as the day in May when he had acquired it. His underwear was a three-piece affair while his socks and garters, such as they were, reached to his knees almost. Nine-tenths nude, he slithered beneath the covers but then immediately came out again when he saw he was lacking any sort of book.

"No book!" he said. "Not even a poor one!"

Thus Lee, who lay for a long time staring up at the assumed location of the ceiling. It was so dark and so cold, so cold and him still so much like what he had always been that he ignited the candle again and searched beneath the bed. Someone had deposited a collapsed ironing board in that space, also a few other random items of no great interest whatsoever. He was not happy. And then, too, there was that noise of the two frogs, a wee one and a greater yelling at each other at a range of two or three hundred rods from the house itself.

He gave it five minutes and then begrudgingly left the bed and reentered his clothes. His collar had cooled during his absence and chilled his neck. He must have wasted another five minutes trying to get his tie into order, and two or three minutes after that, putting his buttons into the assigned holes. It dispirited him to learn that although he had arranged his shoes side by side, he had failed to sequence them in rapport with his feet. Or in other words, that the one shoe was where the other ought to be.

"Goddamn it!" he said, stumbling toward the door and then, next, coming back to take the quilt with him. The mercury had dropped a full nine degrees over the last hours, a worrying transaction that caused the building to contract and speak out against the weather. His blood was too clotted for weather of this sort; nevertheless, he made his way to the entrance of the home and after igniting his candle, hurried back and forth across the yard in an unavailing effort to discover and discontinue the two pestilential frogs.

It proved darker in this direction than in that, nor was it useful to put on his glasses. Even so, he did eventually find the path that led to the house and then the hall that could have carried him back to his room. Instead, he collided into the widow's brother carrying a candle of his own. Both men jumped back.

"Howdy."

"Hi."

"Getting colder, seems like."

"No question about it."

"Thought I saw a great big ole yellow moth trying to get inside."

"You did. But he won't do any harm I don't suppose."

"Already got so many things living in here." (He looked at Lee in a meaningful manner.) And then, in a much quieter voice: "He wouldn't of put up with 'em *for five minutes*, her husband wouldn't. Moths."

"Good man. And frogs?"

"Yep. And snakes."

"Nor reptiles generally, I expect. Well, I think I'll get on back to bed and see if I can't pick up with that dream I was having"

They parted, the brother going in one direction and the old man in quite another. The widow herself had meantime appeared at the far end of the passageway and was standing there with her arms hanging down. Having done all he could for her, Lee smiled encouragingly for the space of a few seconds and then continued on his way.

The sheets were cold. He had cold sheets and another five hours before the sun. "Goddamn it!" he said, removing his shoes and allowing them to drop in random order on the uncarpeted floor. He had no books of course and was resigned to utilizing his heterogeneous memories to pass the time until he might, but probably wouldn't, fall asleep again. He did, however, have access to a radio, a proven household appliance capable of bringing in sounds from hundreds of miles away.

The object, as old and as primitive as it was, was as big as a refrigerator almost. Drawing it astride the bed, he began muddling with the dials, almost at once blundering upon a station somewhere in New Mexico. He discerned that they were promoting a hair lotion of some kind containing, it was avowed, an enriched proportion of lanolin. Coming nearer, Lee pressed his ear to the speaker where he was faintly able to pick up still other voices from even further away. Strange! He could also hear the steady noise of molecules, if that's what they were, coming through the roof and impinging on the speaker. And this: that the human race had been underestimating the magic of these instruments (radio) for far too long. Next, he picked up the blow by blow description of a famous boxing match that had transpired thirty years ago.

He was brought awake by the sound of the radio whispering insidiously in his ear. Imagining he was back in his parents' house, he leapt up and headed off in the wrong direction for the toilet. The place was empty, save only for a small black youth who for the past days had been loitering in the downstairs hall. Repairing to the toilet, he was reminded that this was but a deep hole in the earth with a fifty-pound bag of quicklime at one side. He used it nevertheless and then hastened back to his room in time to stop his shoes from "running away," as his grandmother had enjoyed saying.

He dressed slowly, trying three separate ties before settling upon an unobjectionable one with dark golden stripes. The sun had emerged while he was sleeping but then had come to rest just an inch or two above the horizon. It had a face on it (the sun) that reminded Lee of the Queen of Spades as seen on a certain deck of hundred-year-old playing cards that he had found in an unlikely place in the attic of a person whom he once had known when . . . That's what it reminded him of. The clouds meanwhile looked like protoplasm.

His task for the day was to retrieve his $347 brown suit with the lapels. Pursuant to that, he called for his breakfast and caused the downstairs boy to fetch a pail of water and begin the process of washing his car, which stood in great need of it. This time the coffee was not quite so good as yesterday's whileas for the cream, it bore a curdled look. Lee consumed it anyway and asked for more. Suddenly, he jumped back, dismayed that the woman had *scrambled* the eggs in lieu of the way he liked them. Even then he said nothing, however, not till she went to the oven and brought back a good-looking pie with fork holes in the crust.

"I made this pie," she said. "And we sure do thank you for all the trouble you did. I just know you're going to have a real good time down there at the Gulf and whatall."

They all looked around at each other. It had not occurred to Lee that he might be leaving.

"You can eat it in the car. And look here, here's a great big old spoon you can use."

Indeed, it *was* big, big and made of iron and weighing half a pound he would have said.

"I certainly do appreciate it," said Leland. "Yes, it's time I got back on the road. Don't have a bit of cheese, do you, to go with the pie?"

"I'll help you get packed," the brother offered, rising quickly and heading off toward Leland's room. The man was in overalls and gave the impression that he had passed the morning doing work of some kind. There remained hardly a full half-cup of coffee and it was far from being the best of the brew. Lee helped himself to the toast, a pat of butter, and a layer of cherry jam. At that time, the woman's brother was carrying his suits (Leland's) carrying them one by one to the Fraser. He had, Leland, expected that the car might have been washed by now and was disappointed to find the boy otherwise occupied.

It was still early in the late afternoon and the confusion in Leland's head was at its apex. At first, he thought the car might not function, but after tampering with the controls for a minute or two, the good old motor caught fire and began to move forward taking him with it. In the mirror, he could see the brother and sister scattering to separate places, which is to say the house and barn. The little boy himself was standing in a state of perplexity, a bucket of water dangling from his arm.

He drove steadily for a half-mile or thereabouts and then forced his big iron spoon into what proved to be a blackberry pie. He had no trouble in eating, driving, and thinking at the same time. Fragments of world literature flitted through his mind. He hurried across a bridge too narrow for two cars abreast and reached the opposite shore just as he caught sight of an inactive person floating face up in the current two hundred feet below. There was no cheese on the pie. He tried the radio, charmed to have come in on one of his all-time favorite ballads.

Thus Lee, bending forward in the cockpit with his glasses in his suitcase. It was his plan to stop at the first station, buy fuel, and ask about the young man who had absquatulated with his suit. Was that a service station just ahead on the right-hand side? It was, and when Lee came and parked and gave the four attendants, wastrels all, gave them enough time, he thought, to laugh at his Fraser, that was when he saw that he was being followed by a police car. Lee waved in friendly fashion, trusting to his bumper sticker that expressed a favorable opinion toward law officers in general.

His car needed eleven gallons, a pricy distillate that gave off the sort of fumes that slowly over time had made Lee something of a connoisseur of the stuff. Having paid, he tried to initiate a conversation with the simpleton who appeared to be in charge of the place.

"Clouding up, looks like," Lee said. "And how about that quarterback!" (He was tired, so very tired of having to pretend to be stupid when dealing with Americans.) "Say, you don't know a fellow name of Junior Cobb do you? Short fellow, about five feet five?"

All four men agreed that they did not.

"What'd he do?"

"Well! Seems like he might have my suit, and I might have his."

"No, sir, we don't know where Junior is. Sure don't. He won't be there anyway, this time of day."

Lee paid again, not realizing until six hours later that he had paid already. Probably it was his generosity that persuaded the manager to draw a map for him, a simplified diagram that showed the way to Florida.

Continuing on his way, the old man began to experiment with his Fraser—how fast would it go, etc. Only now did he realize there was a cigarette lighter built into the dashboard. He experimented with this as well, whereupon a considerable smoke began to fill the cockpit. He realized that same patrolman was following hard upon, a thin-faced sort of individual in a kepi and solid black cloak. Lee smiled at him in the mirror and put on responsible facial expression. By this time, his blackberry pie was more than half finished and he was having increased difficulty operating the big iron spoon. Truth was, it had fallen to the floor about five minutes ago. That was why he relocated the pie itself from his lap to the adjoining seat, giving it a more stable position. Meantime, the patrolman had left off following him, abandoning his location to an ostensible farmer in a pickup truck.

The next miles went by normally enough, Lee using the serenity to peruse the roadside advertisements, the mile markers (he was 227 miles from somewhere), and the occasional directional signs that reported the distance to some of the more important places. The sun seemed a little bit smaller than usual, a result of the coefficient of the diffraction, as he explained it. Thus Lee, sailing off to Florida with better than ten gallons in the car, money in his belt, a revolver in a secret place, and long stretches of the world's best music filtering through his head. He had endured a sufficient number of hindrances on this trip and wanted no further ones, apart from what looked like a hitchhiker up ahead.

Lee slowed. It was an Aryan man in need of help, judging from his racial characteristics. Lee slowed further, looking the chap directly in the face.

"Good Lord!" said Lee, noticing the bruises and blood and the other damage that had been wrought upon the fellow.

"Thanks man!" the boy said, racing to the Fraser. "Naw, I really appreciate it! How far you going?"

"Watch it! Don't sit in the pie please. It's got blackberries in it."

"Yes, sir. How far you going?"

"Florida."

"Naw, I don't need to go that far. Matter of fact, the best thing for me is to turn off on Pinesap Road."

"Don't believe I'm familiar with that one, Pinesap. By the way, I notice you've got all sorts of . . . injuries. Altercation, was it?"

"If I could just get to Pinesap, hell I'd be all right then."

"I see. I think I know now why that patrolman was following me. Kill somebody, did you?"

"I don't think so. Maybe. Doubt it. He was still breathing. 'Course now, that was a while ago. Hard to kill, niggers are."

Lee blinked. "Yes, but you had no choice, right? I didn't think so. How far is it, here to Pinesap Road?"

"'Bout ten mile."

Lee put on speed. The highway in front of him was clear, nor did he detect any uniformed men on motorcycles hiding behind billboards. Looking sideways at the boy Lee believed he could detect in him an opera composer, a military hero, a chemical engineer, or something else along those lines had only his life and situation been more favorable than they were.

"Got any family?"

"Used to. Wife ran off to New York."

Lee redoubled his speed. The putative farmer had likewise begun to go faster, spilling corncobs as he moved ever forward. Unable in his ancient car to outrace a General Motors product, Lee opted then to slow and pull over and allow the "farmer" to pass by at eighty miles the hour, as it must have been.

The day was clear and, by southern standards, rather cold. It is true the car had a heater in it, though Lee feared to use it. Turning to the boy, he tried to continue the conversation:

"Enjoy opera, do you?"

"Sir?"

"Bet you were in the military, too."

The boy said nothing. He had a tattoo on the back of his left hand showing a bosomy nude throwing dice. The other hand might also have something on it, except that the boy was using it to staunch what might have been a wound in his lower belly.

"You aren't going to perish on me now, are you?"

"Naw, I'm all right. Don't got any aspirin, do you?"

Lee reached instead for a bottle that two days previously had contained an amount of brandy sealed up tightly with a cork. Today, one could see little tads of that cork floating in the solution. The boy seized upon it.

It proved, proved Pinesap Road, to be a dirt lane, very narrow, that right away conduced up a steep hill where it was almost impossible for an ordinary sedan to gain traction. Lee nevertheless spurted up the incline at his best speed and emerged all at once upon a long level field that stretched far away. It might almost still be 1940 here, judging from the houses and cattle and the two children wrestling in the dust. He had been right, Lee, to rescue a person who belonged to such surroundings as these.

"Which house?" Lee courteously inquired.

"Any of 'em."

"Any?"

"Yeah. We're all kin here."

(Lee could feel his admiration turning to outright jealousy.)

"Must be wonderful, kin. Actually, I think I'll head for that bungalow with the washing machine on the porch." And did so, avoiding the two scarecrows who appeared to be waving at each other across the space.

In cases like this, involving kin, it wasn't necessary to knock on the door. Instead, they pushed into the parlor and laid the wounded boy on a red velvet sofa with embroidered doilies on the arm rests. He had drained the brandy down to almost nothing, had drained the boy, and was giving indications of falling off to sleep. Lee called for help, getting a grandmotherly type with a great-grandmotherly face.

"Needs help," our person revealed. "And I have no further brandy anywhere."

At once she went to work, doing it in such a way as to suggest she had done so before.

"I swear," she said, "it just never stops. Who are you?"

"He's got some serious wounds," said Lee, helping to remove the boy's outer and inner shirts. "That one particularly looks serious to me."

Indeed, it did. It wasn't nearly so much a bullet wound however as a knife's. Lee doused it with the remains of the brandy and tried to plumb the depth of that gash with the smaller blade of his wee pen knife. Standing erect, he now gave his opinion of the affair:

"The knife has not, repeat not, damaged the heart. And the same can be said of the kidneys and liver and all that. As for these minor cuts, ignore them. They really don't amount to anything." Suddenly he jumped back, dismayed to see that six other persons had suddenly and silently manifested themselves in the room. They all of them resembled each other closely, especially about the ears, eyes, noses, and throats.

"Name of Pefley," Lee said, extending his hand for shaking. "Alabama line. Yes, it was hard, and hard on the car, too. But I figured I just had to save him and bring him home to you!"

"Obliged. You a doctor?"

"Ah no, not really, no. Never completed my dissertation. After all, who could have tested me on that particular topic?"

They lifted the boy and spread him out on the floor where they could more easily crowd about. The leader of this bunch appeared also to be the oldest, the proper way for people to organize themselves, Lee believed.

"Lost books of Theopompus. I leave it to someone else to finish what I started."

There were now eight, possibly nine other individuals in the room, all of them still resembling each other to a high degree. Mostly asleep by now, the boy made no complaint when they washed him off and rolled him up in "swaddling clothes," as they called the two somewhat unclean plain linen sheets taken from someone's bed. Lee observed with silent approval as they next daubed an unguent of some nature over the half-dozen minor cuts and abrasions and, finally, the one really important wound.

And now the patient had possession of an inch of brandy, one of Lee's cigarettes, and the tender attentions of a crowd of people who all liked each other.

"So, I guess you all grew up right here on this plot of land," Lee mooted to the man with the newspaper and pipe.

"Pardon me, but I believe that's something we can talk about at a later time. Just now we're worried about Herb."

"Me, too, I'm worried too," Lee claimed, coming forward for another look.

The room had a piano in it together with framed photographs on every possible surface. Putting on his glasses, Lee was able to discern in one of the pictures two persons and a third posing in army uniforms. Suddenly he jumped back, astonished at the image of a family member with a long rifle vaunting over the cadaver of a slain rhinoceros.

"Ach!" he said. "And are there really so many rhinoceri still extant that we can go about murdering the poor things?" (He could feel his gorge rising. Ought he not perhaps have left the boy to rot alongside the highway?)

"Oh, I see" (this said by the man with the salad bowl in his hands), "you're more concerned with rhinos than with Herb. That how it is with you?"

Lee retreated. "No, no, of course not, certainly not, no. For unlike any rhino of my acquaintance, this child here might almost have grown up to be an opera composer!"

"Don't know about that. But he sure was a mighty fine linebacker in his time."

"*In his time*," Lee repeated softly. Himself, he was seventy-eight years old, poor linebacker material, and still waiting patiently for *his* "time" to come along.

Ten

He wasted the next several days poking about in the family's affairs. He might spend the entire morning working at the kiln or creamery, only to repair to the upholstery by afternoon. Fond of parsnips, his favorite winter crop, he must have devoted fifteen hours or more dirtying his suit while digging them out of the cold hard ground. Sometimes, he might assist at the forge or, as part of his long march through the institutions, superintend the illegal growths in the greenhouse that had inspired Herb's name. It wasn't till the third day that he came up against the man named Daniel, the most educated member of the clan. This was and probably still is, a rheumy man full of wattle and dewlap, famous among the family for his collection of little glass giraffes, about two inches high.

"Heat," said Lee, nodding toward the budding plants. "They need far more heat than can be provided by a couple of 1,000-watt lamps."

"Agreed," the man said, broaching up closer to Lee and then, suddenly, jumping back out of range of his cigarette. "But what I really wanted to ask is this."

"Yes?"

"You're a . . . How shall I say? An *elderly* gentleman?"

"True. Southern, elderly. Courtly, too, in some ways."

"And you've been like this for quite some time?"

"I have. Ever since that day back in '59 when I . . ."

"So, if I wanted to know what my own life will be like in, say, twenty-five years from now, I could just ask somebody like you, right?"

"You know somebody like me?"

"Well! Not exactly like you."

"I should think not. Pass me that watering can would you please?"

"See what I mean? 'Would you please?' No, that's wonderful."

"You can't pass a person a watering can without spilling it over his trousers?"

"Sorry."

Lee want back to his task. The plants were developing

flowers that in processed form promised pleasure, he assumed, to certain types of persons. As for himself, he had preferred to die upon the spot than depend upon outside forces for the ecstasy that comes from *internal* riches. He said:

"You people have no fiber, not if you rely on these little blooms, if that's what they are. Hoot man, I don't need blooms, not as long as I have . . ." (He pointed to his head) ". . . this!"

"Well goody for you." And: "It's true that we've had a number of visitors out here over the years, but I do believe you're the most obnoxious one yet."

"Yea, and the only one to have rescued that rash son of yours, who ought to be in the Air Force."

"He tried that."

They fell silent. The boy himself, loaded down with a crate of brown bottles, had just that moment emerged from the distillery. Two dogs followed in his wake. Lee was puzzled by the sight of a much smaller creature of some description mixing with the hounds. Lee:

"How many acres do you actually have out here I wonder. Truth is, we've been looking for investment opportunities of this kind, the woman and I."

The man jumped back, an anguished expression on his face.

"No, sir; no can do. No. We never sell, us. No, we've agreed on that. We like to keep it in our own hands."

"All I'd need is a couple acres."

"No! No, we don't do that. Sorry. No, sir, we prefer to hold on to it."

"And yet, when I think of the good that I could do. Greek, French." (He took on a dreamy expression.) "Did you know I'm considered something of an expert on the Fatimid regime?"

"Yeah, you told us about that. No sir, we're just plain people out here, trying to piece together a living. That's all."

"Yes. The world could end, and you'd still be high and dry. I like that."

"Just trying to survive."

"And why not? After all, in your case your corporeal self is far your best possession. But for me, that's the least of what I have."

"Oh, I don't know, you seem to be in pretty fair shape. For your age."

They gathered that night about the fire in one of the larger homes, a two-story pile with a patriotic weathervane. The old woman (younger than Lee) had opened several jars of canned fruits and vegetables and had set a table worthy of the tables of yesteryear. Taking their fill of fatback and collards, black-eyed peas and squash, the family had poured a dark wine for everyone above a certain age and, picking up where Leland's previous hosts had left off, had begun anew to recite some of the region's favorite stories. Lee took one glass of wine only. Anything less would have been too little, and anything more too much—such was his reasoning in this matter.

Seated on the floor in Indian style, Lee listened with close attention, which is to say until boredom set in. He had spied an afternoon newspaper among the kindling and was eventually able to draw it to himself without causing offence.

So many years had gone by since last he had seen what *Mutt and Jeff* were doing, what new outrage from *Krazy Kat*, or since the media had deigned even to notice the ongoing troubles of *The Yellow Kid*, Lee's favorite of all those people. But first, the stock market news:

Bromine exports had rallied over the period just past.

Moving on hurriedly to political affairs, he learned that a new president had come to power at some point. A friendly-looking sort, the man appeared to be a normal-looking garden-variety human being who gave Lee no immediate opportunity for predicting the demeaning adjectives that later on would be applied to him both by himself and others. But mostly his attention, Lee's, was drawn to the bottom of the page where stood a photograph of a group of well-dressed men (one of them in handcuffs) looking directly back into the camera's orifice.

The following page concerned itself with state and local news, and the one after that with a horrendous mishap in which a contortionist had been strangled in a peculiarly horrible way. Next, he read where a woman had murdered a man. Why? Was it the same old story of love turned to hate, or greed for money, or any of the other matters familiar to us from the ancients? But this was what transfixed Lee, namely that she had used an ice pick. Thinking about that, he shivered violently, calling more attention down upon himself than he wanted. He wadded up the paper and threw it into the fireplace, destroying for the nonce any mention of Mutt or Jeff.

For the past two nights, he had been delegated what was likely the grandest bed (wider than its length) in the entire compound. But not tonight, not after being given an implausible excuse about a certain cousin and his wife expected on the midnight express. Lee, having offered to share the bed, waved it off insouciantly and went cheerfully to the barn where his two suitcases were waiting. It could have been cozy in that loft, had only the mercury been standing about fifteen degrees higher than it stood. Removing his suit and brushing it off and hanging it high, he lay shivering for a certain time before burying himself, most reluctantly, up to his collar in the silage.

Eleven

The whole group turned out for his departure and fluttered him off with large white handkerchiefs. Refusing to weep while still in view, Lee put on a serious look and, bringing his will into play, managed to start his Fraser. They had loaded the car with gifts, most notably fig jelly, home-made whiskey, and half a peck of late peaches that gave off an autumnal small. As for his ruined blackberry pie, it was entirely gone and, in its place, Lee discerned a foot-long sausage taken from the smoke house.

"I must hurry home," muttered Lee to himself, "and show this stuff to Judy." But no, he had promised himself a last look at the great Mexican Gulf, where in old times he had whiled away the second-best summer of his whole career. Meantime, he had lost a good part of his eleven gallons of gasoline, a recurring problem related to incongruities in the fuel line. Holes, in fact. Using his field glasses, he searched for a filling station up ahead where the horizon had "broken down," so to speak, into a discontinuous line of little dots and dashes indicating uncertain boundaries.

This time the radio was playing yet another very good and well-remembered ballad from the 1950s. Lee waited for it to end and then dialed over to a classical station in Tulsa where the music was only intermittently audible between the buildings and hillsides that divided Lee from that city. He had his way, and the world would always be full of the kind of background music accompanying some of our better films. Continuing to have his way, the sky would be bluer than it was, the clouds more tumulus, and each a different color. This was not even to talk about the women, whom no one would dare to look upon without special glasses. Because for Lee it was *beauty* that mattered, horses for example, and stainless oceans analogous to glass. Autumn itself, he said, most agonizing of seasons bringing in its train aubergine leaves as thin as palimpsest. And before death, an "intermission," he went on, when the old were offered to remain here a little longer than they deserved.

He came to his sought-for filling station, passed it by at

forty miles the hour, and then turned and went back for it. Though hardened by now to the sound of laughter, he hated to park in open view. In this instance, it seemed to go on longer than necessary. He grinned sheepishly, put on his self-deprecating face (the only social weapon he still had) and then slipped into his "people's vocabulary" of one- and two-syllable words. "How about that quarterback!" he said. "Looks like rain. Me, I get near about thirty miles the gallon on the highway. Twenty-one in town."

They looked at him through slitted eyes. One man was sitting on the steps, the other in a rocking chair. Deep inside the store, Lee could see a third man nodding in consonance to the sound of a zither on the radio.

"Oil, too, please. If I'm in need of it." And then: "I can pay."

"Looks to me that you're in need of lots of things."

They laughed again, Lee again joining in. He had started to pat the village dog, retracting his pale white hand just in the nick of time.

"And can you tell me the best route to Florida?"

"*Best* route?"

"Why, yes."

"Well, let me see. Best thing, I guess, is start off just *as close as you can get.*"

They all laughed together, Lee prolonging it out of courtesy. He now caught sight of yet a fourth man, an ursine type, more matter than energy, sleeping on the porch.

He received his gasoline and though he had paid for both, got no oil. He also tried to expel the dog from his car but ended up having to sacrifice his sausage. The road ahead discouraged him, nor was he certain it led to Florida. Useless to count the litter that banked the highway on both sides, save to mention how profuse it was. He saw a destroyed baby carriage, a ruined mattress with the feathers coming out, the skeleton of a mule or horse, to put the best interpretation on it. He also keened in upon a country girl walking down a lane, her jeans full of the kind of buttocks that caused him to break out into applause. "Fortunate the lad who takes *her* off to bed!" said he, changing his mind abruptly when she turned at the last moment to expose her face.

At least the cows were handsome enough, however. Judging by them, the time was coming when they must consummate their mission on earth, an honorable estate offering good eating to the nation at large. He then saw a little calf, a dewy creature who hadn't yet been given the details of her brief fate. He saw peanuts yellowing in the field, a small crop of cotton that ought have been harvested two months earlier, and a deserted and leaning farmhouse that had no more than a year or two still remaining to it.

For the past minutes, he had been running parallel with a freight train comprised mainly of sealed cars, some of them listing back and forth rather worryingly he thought. Next, a few dozen passengers passed in review. He locked glances with a thoughtful-looking person who might be somewhat like himself. Came next a child into view, a stupefied individual with its hands pressed against the glass. Lee put on speed, resolved that no mere coal-powered apparatus be allowed to outrun his own personal car. And that of course was when a tank car suddenly exploded, ejecting spumes of a bilious-colored smoke that right away began to settle on both sides of the track.

"Hmm," said Lee, not permitting himself to be distraught by the incident. "Makes it difficult to see, all that chlorine blocking off the view. That stuff can kill you they say, if you let it."

His car had six cylinders, each of them about the size of a soft drink bottle. As the sort of person who preferred always to keep *something* in reserve, he was loath to press the pedal all the way to the floor. And then, too, he couldn't see the road. His whole life, or rather the whole corpus of his readings passed in swift review. Usually, he had wanted his death to come by lightning strike, but this, too, had its appealing side. He tried to recall the amount of his insurance, and the several codicils pertaining to trains and airplanes and the like.

He would split the proceeds between dog charities and a group of archeologists working in the ruins of Gla. As for his personal tomb, he had specified that it have a snorkel that would run a certain distance into the air. Apart from that and Judy, a telephone and a few select volumes of the world's most preeminent literature, he asked but for a pound of cheese, a half-gallon of distilled water, and a few other things of that kind.

His car was ruined, or so he believed as he veered off into a thick (*blessedly* thick) growth of bamboo, some of them bearing little white flowers. Someday, he believed, automobiles would be equipped with straps and bags to ameliorate the sort of concussion he had just now experienced. A balloon-like cushion that could emerge quickly from beneath the dashboard, or even out of the roof itself. Straps, mayhap, like those that surgeons use.

Naw, that would only have added to the cost. Forcing open the door against mediocre resistance, he clambered out into a swale of cane that, as suggested, grew so close together as to have effectively stopped his Fraser. Himself, he was in pretty good shape really, for a man of his years, and had no great problem in coming to ground and getting himself to higher land. Luckily, the poison had by now passed over and appeared to be moving westward.

Shielding his eyes, he watched studiously as some hundred persons came spilling from the coaches, some of them screaming, some wearing facial expressions that he immediately put away in his memory bank. "Chlorides!" he called, doing his best not to laugh. "That stuff can kill you in two minutes!" And then, as if to put frosting on it: "Some of you may be dead already!"

He could walk and chuckle at the same time. Up ahead, he made out the indications of a small town with a hardware store, a water tower, and little else apart from the usual collection of other things. His satchel was full of peaches and fig jelly, shaving equipment and the reissue of an anthology of seventeenth-century pastoral verse. Whistling as he went, continuing sometimes to chuckle, he directed himself toward the hardware store alluded to above. He estimated it at past ten o'clock in the morning, but surely not later than twelve. It couldn't be afternoon, not with the sun the way it was. Great therefore was his embarrassment when at last he checked his watch and apprised himself of the truth.

He had injured his left shoulder. As Leland, he despised pain however, and contented himself by forming a sling from his extensive undershirt. Next, he appropriated a stick that lay nearby, a mere wand really that nevertheless could be used as a crutch of some kind. So equipped, he expected to enter town in full aplomb, indifferent to agony, a limp in his left leg, and blood on his shirt.

He went direct to the hardware store and positioned himself in front of the assumed proprietor of the place, a man who seemed always to be frowning owing to an upside-down moustache.

"This sling," Lee started out, "represents my escape from a train wreck, a literal one, about two miles back." (He pointed.) "Fortunately, I was in my car. A Fraser actually. They used to laugh at me about that."

"You're bleeding."

"Possibly. But that means nothing to me."

"Bleeding on the floor."

Lee looked at the floor, his mind more occupied with something Berdyaev had said than with what lay in front of him. "I do need help," he allowed, "dragging my Fraser out of the shrubbery back yonder; I admit that. You know anyone of that kind?"

"What's a Fraser?"

"Heck, I could probably get by if I just had a fellow with a mule." (He glanced toward a strong-looking individual at another counter, a beefy person of perhaps 250 pounds.) "That one, for example."

"My wife."

"Of course. How about negroes? Got any negroes hereabouts?"

"No, sir. They got one over in Townsonville. Maybe if you could just . . ." (The man had fetched a newspaper, arranging it where the blood was falling. Lee wanted to laugh. He had seen greater blood pools from run-over cats.) ". . . if you could just stand about . . . Here! Good."

In the distance Lee could hear the afternoon bell signaling it was two o'clock. No question about it, time was flying by much faster than of just a few years ago. It urged him to finish his project quickly and get him home again. Speaking too rapidly to be understood, he said:

"I'd be willing to pay, say, twenty-five dollars to anyone who could . . ."

"Sir?"

"Twenty-five dollars."

The woman now spoke up. Her arms, he judged, were as great as a normal person's legs. Putting on his best manner, Lee smiled and listened to what she said:

"Sounds to me like you're pretty well fucked," she said.

"Maybe so. But I'm not abandoning my Fraser. Not now and not ever."

"That's the spirit! Okay, tell you what I'll do."

Lee waited for the rest of the information which, however, never arrived. Meantime, another customer had entered the place and was inquiring frantically and irrationally for a stretcher or wheelbarrow, for oxygen tanks and as many first aid kits as the store could supply.

"Fifty dollars—that's my highest bid," Lee said, casting his eyes on the stranger.

"Fifty?"

"Yes siree. Fifty. Green dollar bills."

"What do I got to do?"

"Drag my car out of the sugar cane. I'd do it myself, if I'd gotten enough sleep."

He was a child, the stranger, who hadn't yet seen his fortieth year. He *was* hefty-looking however, the sort of person who could bear up under a harness and reins. Leaving the wheelbarrow, they headed off in the direction whence Lee had come and, to make a tedious narration short, liberated Leland's only slightly disfigured car. Unsuccessful at bargaining with the fellow, Lee passed over the full amount and after putting his possessions (suits, fishing tackle, jelly) into better order, leapt out onto the highway and ran away.

He drove steadily for the best part of half an hour. It was a bleak area and he began to understand why the map hadn't troubled to announce any of the very few details in evidence. He passed a kaolin operation (abandoned) standing out in the middle of nowhere, also an industrial-scale suntan salon with perhaps a hundred automobiles parked all about. Except for that and a city on the right-hand side, Lee had one reason only—oil, gas, and water—for coming to a stop.

The laughter had crested and died away almost before he had exited his car. In this case, the attendants were nondescript persons, giving Lee no leverage for putting them in his memory bank.

"I'm interested in the quickest way to Florida," he said, getting and expecting no answer to what really wasn't a question after all. He stood in need of water (water for the battery and water for cooling), also oil, fuel, and transmission fluid. To pay for these essential liquids, Lee handed over yet another fifty dollars, receiving in exchange two paper bills and a quantity of pocket change, some of it of Argentine origin he believed. Saying nothing about that, he strode up to the smaller attendant and asked the question that had been bothering him for the past four days.

"What's the best way to Argentina, please? No! *Florida* I mean."

The man laughed out loud at him, an unlikeable sight that revealed the man's dental plight. "Well what's it going to be? 'Sir.' Argentina or Africa?"

Lee laughed jovially. "Florida. The reason I said 'Argentina' was because . . ."

"Well sir, Florida is a powerful big place. You got your Miami, you got your Tampa. Got lots of other places, too."

"No, actually it's the *Gulf* I'm interested in." (Again, he had technically failed to ask an actual question.)

"Interested in the Gulf," the fellow yelled to his partner.

"Is?"

"Yeah. He dudn't say why, just says he's interested."

"Be careful. You never know about these people."

"No, no," laughed Lee. "I'm a perfectly respectable human being, and all I want . . ."

"Bleeding, too."

"Christ. Get rid of him if you can."

The first man now turned back to Lee, saying:

"Miami, that's what I recommend. You got your Spanish type people down there, your Jigaboo Americans, your homosexual queers. Finest people in the world."

"I see."

"You got your ocean and all that sun. That's what I'd do."

Lee thanked the man fulsomely. Only a few minutes, emotionally speaking, had passed since last he had examined his watch, and yet he had lost almost another full hour of his wasting tenure in southeast Alabama.

Twelve

The landscape continued apace. Keeping a bright eye

out for his fluids, Lee hurried past a tiny town conspicuous for the number of patrolmen waiting in ambush. Never would he have been able to outrun these people, preferring instead to proceed very slowly while wearing an emollient smile. Already he had caught sight of the next city on his route, a place of stark white buildings framed against a cerulean sky. It seemed to betoken a true civilization, a place for sculptors and ambulating philosophers instead of the cultural democracy actually on offer.

He moved slowly among pornographic theaters, lottery outlets, sixteen clothing stores for women and one for men. He viewed a drunk man peeing in the gutter and then a combined bookstore and bowling alley vending cotton candy and diet aids. The air was full of primitive music interrupted only by the sporadic announcement of basketball scores. He saw a hermaphrodite with an apparatus strapped to his shaven head. Continuing the inspection, he perceived any number of very heavy but also very calm-looking adults waddling forward in sandals and unclean shorts, many of them dressed in T-shirts with gnomic captions on them. Passed a woman devouring a foodstuff of some sort as she drifted at random down the walk. And yet, the buildings were tall, blanche, and lean. Lee had to ask: Had ever there been a society where the people and their technology were qualitatively so distinct?

Never, and when he pulled into the next station to "top off," as was said, his gasoline fuel, and had held up his hand to warn away the laughter, and had peed (going to the right place for doing that) he asked:

"Know of a good place to eat?"

"Well," the person said sleepily, "around here, we don't actually eat places. But we do got the *Shrimp Palace*, the *Hamburger Hullabaloo*, the *Happy Belly*, the . . ."

Lee stopped him. The man was seemingly blind and accepted without demur two of our man's foreign dimes. What he wanted really, Lee, was a family restaurant for the lower bourgeoisie, a place with little or no music and a southern waitress to call him "darling," if not "honey" indeed.

And found it down among the stews where a great many embryonic insects had taken lodging in last week's rainwater. Entering with average aplomb, he posed briefly in the doorway and then paced quickly to the further booth provided with salt and pepper shakers and pepper but no salt. Unfortunately, there was a jukebox in the corner; fortunately, it hadn't been activated. The waitress proved exactly what he had craved, a thirty- or forty-year-old woman who had been through two or three marriages and had mostly given up on that sort of thing. Her breasts, however, were still relatively good, and he could reconstruct the nipples beneath her tunic.

"Excellent!" he said. "For a long time now, I've had nothing but coffee and pie, but what I'd really like, sweetheart, is a great big . . ."

"You're bleeding."

"Oh, not really. Or not seriously anyway. Besides, it doesn't mean anything to me, stuff like that. The kind of person I am."

"I'll get you some mercurochrome."

He submitted to it. The woman was calm and, incredibly, seemed actually to be applying her inborn maternal instinct to a seventy-eight-year-old hound with blood on him. Despite her worn-out persona, he again glanced to her two well-formed bosoms that, although not of his very favorite size, nevertheless failed to repel him.

"You need to be more careful darlin'. And look at you, you've gone and ruint this great big old suit!" (She tested the fabric between her forefinger and thumb.) "I'll bring you some coffee dear, and then we can figure out what else we ought to have."

Again, he submitted to it. Apart from himself, there were some eight or maybe ten other mediocrities huddled among the tables. This is what he liked, a room of depressed people who had nothing to say. He focused upon a widower, as he presumed, who really had no good reason to go on much longer. His children had long ago given up on him, he needed a new roof on his three-room house, and his truck was going out. Lee made an effort to win his attention and having succeeded, gave him a full-throated smile which however seemed rather to nonplus the fellow than to cheer him. It never failed; our man had only to smile at a person in order to have him or her, especially her, get up and walk away.

He was brought a pint and half of coffee in a capacious cup. Lifting out his pharmaceuticals, Lee now removed the six several caps and tossed down an elongated pink capsule that appeared to have recently been leaking. Most of the pills were white of course, the world's most exhausted color, as Melville had long ago remarked. One of the medicines was sweet and one was not, which helped Lee decide which of them to chew and which not. And then there was that blue sucker, the one that was supposed to support the limbic system.

"Gosh," she said. "Where'd you get all them pills?"

"Paid dear for them. Want one?"

She laughed and backed off, but then came forward again.

"What would it do for me?"

"Make you even more beautiful than you are."

"Oh, it will not! Which one?"

"Pink one."

She bent over the pill and examined it at close range. Someone had allowed a dog into the place. Lee approved of this. Apparently the South was not yet altogether dead. Outside a policeman walked past, halted, came back, and then pressed his face against the glass. Lee smiled. His waitress had meanwhile reappeared with a slice of gooseberry pie, the result of a misconstruction of his actual request. Even so, he threw it gladly into his waiting maw and banged several times on his cup with his fork to summon the woman back to him.

"Excellent," he said. "Wonder if I couldn't also have a bit of meatloaf, gravy on it, potatoes. Biscuit and butter; you understand."

She wrote it down. Her apron was badly stained and very ugly, wherefore Leland willed himself to think of other things, fragments of literature for example. He still needed to force down one more pill, a moldy item with whiskers on it. "Oh good," he said. "Who needs food when I can get all the proteins I need by this means alone?" He then drew out his second-hand copy of Procopius and spread it flat. It did give him a sort of malicious pleasure, finding that his own historical period was not altogether history's worst.

He left the place at about three o'clock, went a distance, and then circled back to observe his waitress as she seized upon the pink pill and the enormous tip he had left behind. Glancing upward, he caught sight of an egg-like cloud, its yoke the sun. By no means was it too early to be looking for shelter, hopefully with a dedicated bathroom and a two-quilt bed. Pursuant to that, he stopped a very short and somewhat raniform pedestrian of about 155 pounds and asked about the matter.

"Wonder if you could tell me . . . "

"Probably. But you need to calm down just a little bit."

"I'm calm! I'm nearly always calm!"

"Yes? But why are you jumping up and down like that? Maybe you need a prescription. Bleeding, too. No, I'm just trying to be helpful."

Lee jumped up, but then immediately came down on his feet and stayed there. "Well, it's a pretty strange town you have here I must say. Everybody real calm all the time. What's the story about that?"

The man looked away, as if trying to decide whether to

tell. "We're into serenity here. That's all."

"Me, too, I like it, too, be damned if I don't!"

"There you go again. I can't talk to you."

Lee kept still. There must have been twenty very pacific-looking persons ambulating up and down the sidewalk, a population of lotus eaters it seemed. "Okay, I'll keep still. I promise."

"I don't know."

"I said I'd keep still, goddamn it! And anyway, you still haven't even told me where to spend the night!"

Three-and-a-half minutes now went by, a sufficient time for Lee to control himself and for the two of them to draw off into the cavity formed by the display windows of a woman's clothing store. Lee accepted the man's offer of a cigarette and in return gave away one of his own.

"There's a reason people in this town are so stable, I believe you said."

"Yes. Of course."

"Makes me curious."

"Obviously."

"Something in the water?"

They laughed, both. Followed then the actual story:

"It all started a long time ago. Bad economic times. Three suicides in one week. Exports were down. Appeared among us then a certain Dr. ------------" (He refused to give the name).

"And?"

"Takes care of us real good, that one does."

Lee came closer. The window had half a dozen manikins in it together with a true woman (very calm) moving back and forth. Never had Lee witnessed so much peace and quiet among so high a percentage of the people. "You can tell *me*," he said. "What, does he keep the town on drugs, or something?"

"Absolutely not! No, sir! He doesn't hold with drugs."

"What then? Sure do wish you'd tell me."

"Well, I suppose it would be all right. Seeing what kind of person you are."

"Certainly, it's all right! Look at me!"

"Got blood on your shoe."

"We were talking about Dr. ------------!"

"Easy now. Take it easy. Okay, let me put it this way: you got troubles, he'll give you a prefrontal. Sixty dollars is all he asks."

Lee jumped back.

"Ask any of these taxi drivers around here. They'll take you to his place over on ---------- Street." (He declined to name the street.)

"Blimey!"

"Doesn't take him more than ten minutes neither. Hell, I went on my lunch hour."

"Works real fast does he?"

"Fast, cheap, and it doesn't hurt hardly any at all."

"Fast and cheap. Interesting."

"Okay, we had this one case last year. But hell, she was already half-dead anyway."

"Probably would have died anyway. Interesting, interesting."

"But you got to keep quiet about stuff like this. We got us a small town here, know what I mean?"

"I do. No, I noticed how small and peaceful it is when I first came driving in."

"*Real* small."

"That's a true fact—small."

"People talk, you know."

"Not I."

"Mrs. --------- runs a boarding house over on ---------- Street. You might give her a try."

That woman, though peaceful and mild, proved to be a glandular type appareled in a cotton dress. Lee offered her a cigarette and tried to shake with her. "I'm on my way," he said, talking slowly if not in fact condescendingly, "to Florida."

"Everybody his own drummer."

"And I require a room for just one night."

"All full up. What, somebody stick a knife into you?"

"Ha! No, no, I'm not bothered about stuff like that."

"Bothers me."

"Well, how about a couch, or even just a flat place on the floor? I am just truly exhausted, really." (He put on a pathetic appearance.)

"All my rooms are flat! Well, I could put you in with Sherry I guess."

Lee jumped back.

"He's a man," she claimed.

"Ha!"

"Used to be anyway. Where's your luggage?"

Lee pulled out his Procopius, showed it, and then pointed to his automobile.

"That your car?"

"Yes, ma'am!"

They laughed in unison. The sun was doing poorly, and soon now Lee expected to hear his beloved whippoorwills iterating in the glade.

This "Sherry" turned out to be both calm and ambiguous at the same time. Lee took note of his black lipstick, the cosmetics scattered about, and the photograph on the wall of a well-known weightlifter in a metallic brassiere. Lee smiled expansively and held out his hand to shake with it, a nice gesture that was *not* returned.

"Seems like you could at least shake with me."

"This room is too small as it is! And I'm having some friends over later on."

"'Friends?'" He grimaced, Lee, then put on his hat and took his leave. The landlady, smiling broadly, stood waiting for him.

"This is not for me," our man said. "Mayn't I have my rent money back? Fifteen dollars?"

"Sorry."

Lee growled. There was a large man in her apartment and neither she nor he had been to Dr. -----------, of that much Lee felt certain.

"All right, could I have *half* of it back?"

In the end, he was given three dollars and sent upon his way. He found two urchins trying to get into his car and, opening the door, found a third person with his finger in the jelly. Very little still remained of his gooseberry pie or, indeed, his braking fluid. Even so, he managed to start the engine and push forward for about two hundred rods. Suddenly, he jumped back, startled by the representation of a fourth child in the rearview mirror. It was due precisely to such events as these that he had been meditating his own visit to Dr. ------------ but had changed his mind when he bethought him that he might need all his faculties for the books he still hoped to read. Instead, he ignited one of his Egyptian cigarettes and watched as the fumes sank down around his shoes.

It needed only a short drive to carry him to *Acragas*, an entrenched town located where no sane person would have agreed to place it. Formed of brick and other litter, a thirty-foot wall encircled the place entirely. Here, Lee could identify where an ancient aqueduct still provided the potable water the place required. As to the gate itself, (guarded solely by a superannuated man with a dog and horn), it was a frail and rusted-looking thing that had not probably been needed for a very long time. Leaving his Fraser and approaching on foot, Lee revealed that he was going to Florida, that he was behind schedule, and that he yearned to rejoin his wife. Peering over the ledge, the watchman said:

"She'll be in Florida then, your wife?"

"No, no; she never goes abroad anymore."

"Hmm. Well maybe you should be more like her. I can't let you in here, not at 9:40 at night."

"It's true that I should have been more like her."

"You bet." And then: "Hey! Where'd you get that car? I just love those old things. And that suit!"

Lee smiled anyway. "I'm wondering: How long actually before you do open the gate?"

"For you?"

"Yes, for me!"

"Okay, we might let you in. But not that kid in the back seat, you can't expect that."

Lee looked into the back seat, astonished to find two urchins sleeping nose to nose among his rods and reels. He was sucking his thumb, one of them, while the other appeared to be suffering from dreams. He needed only a few moments, Lee, to abandon the cockpit and deliver them out into the world.

"Hee!" quoted the *douanier*. "All right, I'll let you in now, you've earned it."

But even then, it required an unusual time for the apparatus to put itself into gear and for the gate with many a creak and groan begin at last to open. Ahead, Lee saw the crux of the downtown city, including a run-down hotel under state control and, just next to that, a sixteen-story Federal structure with a saying of Orwell's running around the architrave. Driving with absolute discretion, he moved slowly past a clutter of youths standing uselessly in front of a cinema that had closed down years before. A very long time since last Lee had seen a Gail Russell film, and it had an emotional effect on him to see her name still posted on the marquee. Strange, no, how so appealing a woman could have been reduced by now to some twenty-weight of bone? He hated the very nature of things.

Apart from that and the wastrels loitering in front of the theater, the town was sealed up for the night. He drove slowly past a domestic residence where a dim light was glowing darkly in one of the rooms. There, lying in comfort under a vicuña covering, an as-yet uncorrupted couple was gazing deeply, very deeply indeed, into one another's eyes. Next door, meanwhile, another couple who no longer loved each other very much was copulating strenuously on a stained box-spring mattress with some of the cotton sticking out—such was Lee's diagnosis of matters in the town called ------------.

In his youth, Lee had aspired to become a totalitarian dictator but gradually had lost that desire as he came to understand the essence of human beings. "There can be no honor," he said, "in lording it over such things as that." And: "Why one might as well maintain an amoeba farm!" Instead, he had focused upon turning himself into a superior being in the Nietzschean sense, a project that had required him more than three and a half weeks.

But he still needed a place in which to sleep. Sick of hostels and flat places, he aimed for a lofty building that just might be the town's best hotel but then continued on past when he found it was a jewelry store for women. Came next a late-night church with a pastor in the door, and then a nursing home, a distribution point for government cheese, a self-esteem training center, a gym and suntan salon, two video rentals, a union hall for Elvis imitators, a Buddhist temple, and other ingredients of the local economy. Unluckily he, Lee, had begun bleeding again. He cared less than nothing for such details but conceded to popular opinion by pulling into the emergency entrance of a respectable-looking building with a caduceus hanging over the door. Lee goes inside.

"Yes, sir?" (This said by a cheerful receptionist dressed in make-up and a skirt too short by much for her 4'9" form. It was, in other words, that dress, about four inches long.)

"Thought I'd stop by," Lee said. "Nice place you have

here. I'm bleeding."

"Oh! I'll say! And need some pills as well!"

Bored already, he besat himself in the vestibule and began thumbing through some of the really inane magazines deemed of interest to typical patients. (That was before he noticed the most recent emission of the *Tongue and Groove Society*, as they had shamelessly named themselves.) Better would have been a pool table for the customers, or chess set, or a tiny but select library of Greek and Roman classics. Instead, he squandered perhaps ten minutes reading of redecoration strategies for suburban dining rooms.

Another patient had got there before him and was waiting much nearer the door. Not only that, the fellow had seized upon the best magazine in the whole place, a glossy product showing a caught bass leaping into the air. After offering the man a cigarette and then returning it to the package, Leland said:

"I caught me a bass like that one time. Is it serious, the reason you're here?"

The man turned slowly and looked at him. "Where?"

"Tallapoosa River. 'Course, I'm not saying it was *that* big. Pretty big, but not that big."

"I used to fish the Tallapoosa. Mostly just caught eels."

"Bad luck. You need to see the doctor right away I expect. Me, I could die just while sitting here."

The man looked about and then bent closer, whispering: "Try the Chattahoochee."

"I dare say!"

"We use dynamite, my brother and me. Shit, we got us enough bass back in October to last the whole year. Maybe more."

"Really! But that's illegal, isn't it? Dynamite?"

The man looked at him strangely, got up slowly, and relocated to the other side of the room. It gave Lee the position he wanted, making him the next in line.

The "doctor," or "general practitioner" actually, was an irate man with a knobby head that looked like a dozen tennis balls glued together.

"Bleeding," Lee said.

"Yes. And I suppose you can't afford to pay me either. That's why you're here."

"Pay? You wouldn't say that if you could see the sort of car I drive."

"Show me."

They went together to the window.

"Not that old Ford?"

"Would it were! No, my car is that seasoned Fraser you see yonder."

"Kaiser actually. My granddaddy had one like that."

"See? You wouldn't charge *him* now would you? No."

"You people. Okay, take your clothes off and hop up on that table. I realize it's cold up there."

Lee did get onto the table but declined absolutely to remove his apparel. Bored, he watched with indifference as the aide rolled his (Leland's) left sleeve, causing both men to jump back. It was the first time Lee had exposed the dread wound that he had been carrying around.

"Christ, you could have died out there in the waiting room! Why didn't you say something?"

"'Cause I can't pay," said our man pathetically.

"God A'mighty, that's deep. Here, look here and you can see the bone!"

"Not getting squeamish on me, are you? Anyway, I've seen lots of bones in my day."

"Jesus. Okay, I'm going to put some stuff in there and sew you up. You'll need a shot first. And anesthetic."

Lee could not but laugh. "Anesthetic? No, thank you; I won't need that, people like me."

"Oh, Jesus H. Christ; don't tell me you're one of those *Nietzsche* people, for Christ sakes."

Lee blushed. It represented the first time, to his

knowledge, that a trained person knew ought of such matters. It put him in a situation in which he couldn't really protest the two several injections foisted on him at that time. As to the injury, he chose rather to focus on certain excerpts from German literature. Meantime, the charitable physician, a fraudster if ever Lee had seen one, filled his wound with a grease of some brand and sealed it up with clips and very fine wire.

They chatted briefly, up until the "doctor" began to take an interest in some of Leland's more conspicuous quiddities.

"Going to Florida, you say. Why?"

"The Gulf of course. Wanted to see it just one more time."

"I don't believe that car of yours will go that far."

"I know that!"

"And, you've lost a good deal of blood."

"Very well, how far *will* it go, since you know so much?"

"And look at that shirt, if that's what it's supposed to be. Far too thin for this time of year."

Oh, for God's sakes. That kind of stuff means nothing to me. Nothing! Also, I have no place to sleep in." (He held back the tears.)

There happened to be one last patient in the vestibule, an overweight negress who, the doctor explained, liked to frequent this and other clinics in return for the attention she was able to glean.

"Look at that. Fat, stupid, lazy. And I'm supposed to give her a Federally-sponsored enema twice a week."

Lee held up his hand but the doctor went on talking:

"You assume she's poor, yes?"

"Well, I . . ."

"Wrong. She's richer than either of us. Especially you."

"But . . ."

"Wrong. She has put together so many benefits and allowances, so many provisions and benisons and sops, she grosses—no pun intended—more than my best nurse!"

"Is that the truth? How does she do it? And how could I . . ."

"She's passing."

"Passing?"

"Passing as black. You could do it, too, if you wanted to go to that academy over in Fleeceberg."

"Academy, you say."

"Bunch of English professors. *They'll* teach you how to pass."

Lee jumped back, a habitual but unconsidered act that very nearly caused him to drop off the operating table. "A dismal story, but still I have no place to sleep in."

The physician drove in a northerly direction, Lee following closely behind. He almost thought the man was trying to lose him in the traffic, until at last he relented and permitted Leland to close the gap. His car tag also had a caduceus on it, a tiny emblem in the upper right corner just next to the Masonic sign.

And so, they continued on through rich and poor neighborhoods, finishing in an expansive demesne identifiable as upper caste by the goldfish ponds and Grecian statuary. Lee parked carefully between a group of pink flamingos on one side and a black yard jockey on the other. He had the suspicion that the doctor had again forgotten him, wherefore Lee put on speed and actually got to the door before him. The wife—and Lee liked her at once—had good skin and feet but spotted teeth. Unhappily, her head was much like her husband's, albeit composed of fewer spheres.

"Pefley," he said. "Coffee County branch."

They shook. It was a modern kitchen with two refrigerators, a chop block, and a set of horn-handle steak knives of all various lengths. Feeling quite certain that he was soon to be offered a drink, Lee drifted to the main room and selected a blue velvet armchair that conformed suitably to his own person. But remained there only briefly before he caught view of two fairly interesting paintings and a really yummy collection of brown and blue books.

It was dark in that room, but the books themselves had been organized with proper attention to color and size. Right away, Lee's attention was caught by the Estienne edition of Rintelheim's *Memoirs*, perhaps the most disgraceful set of confessions in a century that was famous for them. "I've changed my mind about you," Lee said loudly, aiming his remark at the doctor.

"Glad to hear it."

The better to make out the gold-framed portraits in that room, Lee put on his glasses, very nearly leaping out of his skin when he descried the official 1878 portrait of Wagner in his velvet hat. His host had come to join him meanwhile, bringing with him at long last the drink Lee had wanted. He still had to fight for it however.

"Aren't you drinking?" Lee asked.

"I guess not." And then: "Still bleeding a little bit, aren't you? The rug."

"Wagner! Back in '40, my old father-in-law saw Melchior in the flesh. Doing *Parsifal*."

The practitioner jumped back. "*Parsifal* you say?"

"Yes."

"Interesting, interesting. No, I would have taken you for a *Ring* man. If even that."

"I respect the *Ring*, but I froth for *Parsifal*."

They looked at each other, each man searching the other's eyes for the assumed underlying quality.

"And so, you're a Parsifalist after all?"

"Bet your ass."

"My, my, my. So you say. You knew of course that I have a pirated copy of Syberberg's film."

"Say what?"

"No question about it. I have it, and it's mine."

Lee limped back to his favorite chair, sat for a while, and then called for another drink. "But do you have the requisite machine," he inquired, "wherewith to play the thing?"

"I do. But are you up for it? And in the right spiritual frame?"

"I'll need a bath of course," Lee confessed. "But except for that . . ." (Again, he almost abandoned his skin, the result of the man's woman bending inadvertently over the couch in exactly the way he would have demanded if he were paying for it.) ". . . except for that."

In fact, he bathed twice, Leland, and borrowed the physician's razor to take off his three-day growth of beard, a lichen-like manifestation of a net average length of about a quarter-inch. Having accomplished that, he resorted to his Kaiser for a fresh suit and socks and an after-shave lotion with a woodland scent. The woman, he noted, was standing at her vanity, working conscientiously on her lipstick and make-up and eyebrow pencil. Lee had no criticism of that, this eternal attempt by women to turn themselves into *objets d'art*; on the contrary, he actually cheered for them, urging them always to greater efforts.

"Gosh!" he said, "You really are a handsome woman, and never mind how old you are. Wagner would be pleased."

She smiled briefly, blushed, and then exited her boudoir and closed the door behind her. She really was good-looking, and yet Lee was mindful of what his response might have been had he not already been familiar with the species—the head attached by a stem, funny elbows, a hidden endoskeleton compressing her glossy organs. The "doctor" meantime had mixed three drinks, had disconnected the telephone (a commonplace appliance by that date), and had drawn all the curtains save the one that looked out upon a blinking purple and green neon sign that had an attraction of its own. It was then the three people came together in the center of the room, touched hands, and then went to their respective places.

Six weeks had gone past since Lee had last faced up to that opera's overture, an ascending "staircase to paradise" in the composer's patented style. Too late to cancel the production, he covered some of his face with his napkin and pretended that he was calm, more or less, and merely an interested spectator, as he liked to be seen. Confident that he *could* stand up to the first and second acts, already he was beginning to dread the third and with it the good likelihood that he might disgrace himself in front of a decent-looking woman in a silvery gown.

Thirteen

He woke at just after noon and waited for about ten minutes for the coffee that never came. Nor did he admire his assigned room, a place of storage full of old dust-covered furniture and travel-worn trunks of which all but one couldn't be opened. Last night's music had not quite faded away as yet, and he perforce teetered back and forth perilously for a few seconds before coming to balance. Was it the smell of real toast and eggs wafting up to his attic chamber, or purely a mental construct in which he was put into communication with the eggs and toasts of his youth?

Robed in his clothes, he went downstairs as quietly as possible in the hope of picking up some of the husband-and-wife conversation taking place just then in the kitchen. Trivia was what he heard. Clothed in his robe (as he should have said), he then stepped suddenly into view and addressed his hosts:

"G'morning! Sleep well? I did. Except for that last movement I mean."

"Care for a cup of coffee?" (This from the woman.)

Lee waved it off, but finally relented after all. "Cream

and sugar, too." (They were constantly being interrupted by the *television*, a twentieth-century implement found in the homes of all social classes. The announcer in this case was a blond woman of exceptional beauty who seemed to Lee too young to know any great deal about politics and news. He turned it off.)

"These events," he said "are but the precipitations of ordinary common-denominator human behavior. Hell, I was already young when I recognized how politics is overborne by human nature." (He drank. The stuff was hot but not very good, the beans having perhaps not been evenly ground.) "The public life can be only so good therefore, which is to say not very good at all. Our job, yours and mine, is to turn away from all that, from politics and banking and alliances and everything else of that kind."

"But not medicine, I hope."

"Turn away I say. Happiness, too; it's just not worth the attentions of a serious man."

"Apart from being impossible you mean?"

"No, really, you should try to be more like me—an all-seeing mind floating through space."

"The view! And what should I be thinking about up there?"

"Wisdom, think about wisdom. No! Think about beauty; that's so much better."

"Strange man, aren't you?"

Clothed at last in his clothes, Lee met the man at the door and joined him in the car. A motorist had been injured in the west part of town and it was the doctor's obligation to proceed to that location and do what he could. All his life, Lee had wanted to render aid and then walk away without acknowledgement. Thus, had it been with old Epaminondas, reduced to the ranks for having saved his country.

"They didn't much like him," said Lee apropos of nothing. "But they couldn't do without him!"

"I suppose not."

Three automobiles had collided at the intersection of Jackson and Harvey Oswald. A man was holding to a traffic sign, bleeding at the head. Lee leapt from the car and went instead to the worst of the injuries, the one belonging to a youth of some twenty or thirty years. The boy had lost an eye and part of his forehead but had remained conscious all the same. Lee was not especially horrified, not after all the fiction he had read about wars and their effects. Getting down on one knee he listened to what the child was saying:

"Not going to make it. Am I?"

"You might. Anyway, who knows what lies on the other side? Heck, you might like that even better!"

"Awesome."

Lee was about to say more but was pulled away and lifted up and pushed to one side by a studious-looking medic in a white uniform. Lacking further duties, our man began prudently to pick his way among the wreckage, sometimes gathering up various artifacts of historical value and adding them to his satchel. He passed over the little variegated shards of glass, so many it seemed as if the road were sprinkled with rough-cut diamonds ranging in size from the very tiny up to the much more sizeable. It still didn't amount to much, aesthetically speaking, and after Lee had surveyed the full scene, he began to fall into the sort of ennui familiar to him from all the other times when he had wanted to be doing something else.

"Ready to go?" he asked, going to his host and tugging at the man's shoulder. (Shoulder because the man was on his knees.) "You can't do any more for that little fellow." (On his knees because the physician still was fussing over what had turned into a full-blown cadaver by now.) "Besides, that kid may be in paradise for all we know. Or the equivalent of that."

They drove back slowly to the doctor's house and the still unfinished pot of coffee. Both men had blood on them, though Lee's was mostly his own. Already the sun was nudging up behind the buildings, revealing the silhouettes of all sorts of flautists and guitarists playing on the rooftops to call the sun into view. Lee dasn't gaze into that dangerous orb for better than a few seconds, just time enough to exercise his will upon an object as far away as that. Said the doctor: "If you don't stop with this *now*, you're going to end up not able to tell your imagination from the truth."

"Too late," Lee said.

But they'd not gone more than a dozen blocks before they began to run into scads of working people striding off anxiously to their working places—office buildings and the like. Lee could not find a single face in that procession that hadn't preferred to be at home and in bed, surrounded by books and coffee cups. Why did they do it then, this diurnal madness that, yes, might provide them with ten-room houses someday when Daphnis and the others had been just as well sufficed with two? When once they rode on horses in lieu of metal vehicles that had left the county strewed with body parts? When once the world had just one man per thousand acres rather than the other way around?

The woman, it turned out, was waiting in the yard. Disappointed that she had put herself into ordinary street clothes, Lee nevertheless went toward her smilingly, confident she had brought the coffee with her. Imagine his dismay when he saw that his Fraser had been turned about in such a way that it pointed *toward* the avenue rather than as he had left it. Apparently, these people imagined he was on a tight schedule and wouldn't be able to sojourn with them any longer. He could not but laugh at their mistake.

The day was bright and sunny, also clear and honeysuckled. He was quite calm despite the evidence of villages burning at the extreme border of his historical periphery. He passed a dilapidated home with a person dangling from the rafters. How strange it was! that he alone was able to read these drear haruspications of the times to come. The earth, too, was in decay. He drove by a magnolia orchard, the trees having lost their quondam blooms. And whereas at one time a person could expect to find negroes in overalls trundling hopelessly down the highway, now they dashed past him in foreign cars. He cursed.

This time, he really was going south, to judge from a roadside sign with the word written on it. Already, the vegetation was changing into more primitive things, conifers for example, dating from the Silurian Age. He passed a mule-powered wagon loaded to the gunnels with coconuts, and then drew up with a multicolored lizard of great size running shoulder to shoulder with him down the highway. Came next a swampy terrain full of insect-eating flowers that gave off a seductive smell.

His excitement increased. It is true that a discontinuous trail of leaked gasoline continued to chase up behind him, and yet his was a noble-looking car, more tested than those of others, and it chagrined him to see college students and others of that kind racing past him at twice his own velocity. Suddenly, just then, he acknowledged the boundary line between Alabama and Florida, a bright golden stripe that ran across the road and continued on to an unoccupied shack situated just next to a burnt-out tractor. Lee got out and pulled over and, oblivious to the tourists hurtling by, seized up a fistful of sand and smelt of it. All his Alabama misdemeanors fell now into full abeyance, fading ink on forgotten documents in another jurisdiction altogether.

He continued forward for perhaps a thousand rods and then, even as his fuel ran out, coasted into a filling station where stood a man tempting the tourists with an array of memorabilia piled next to the road. There was no question but that the fellow had absorbed too much sunlight, as proved by his complexion and scales possibly.

"Really, you ought to be wearing a hat," Lee suggested.

"This *is* a hat!"

They fell silent, listening to faraway foghorns coming over the sea. The man was old, nearly as old as Lee, wherefore our man's opinion of him took a more positive turn. That was the moment when someone, a college student belike, threw an empty beer can in their direction. Infuriated at that behavior, Lee raced to the Fraser and loaded his .357 as quickly as he could. Thus Leland, debating whether to kill the next student who came along, as fungible as they were.

He filled the car with premium gasoline and then retreated to the rear of the station to be safe from the projectiles aimed in his direction. The attendant had been using this area for an outdoor "bathroom," as Lee noted with disgust. The temperature at this latitude in November was in the sixties and seventies for the most part, good weather for fishing and swimming.

"Looking forward to getting down to the coast," Lee admitted. "I want to see the Gulf one last time. Fish and swim."

The man chortled and looked away. "Fish?"

"Why yes."

"Oh, my Lord, there ain't no fish down there! Not since that G.O. business."

"Oh. Well, I thought I might try anyway. G.O.?"

"Yep."

"Real bad is it? All that G.O.?"

"Bad as you could want it. Worse."

"I see." And then: "Technically speaking, what *is* G.O. actually? In general, I mean?"

"Grey Ooze! Where you been all this time?"

"Well, I . . ."

"Okay, some people call it *Grooze*, don't you know. It's like this: They started out calling it Grey Ooze, and then they called it Grooze. Next thing, they was calling it just G.O., plain and simple. But they already had a G.O. in the Defense Department, so they started calling it Grey Ooze again. That's what I do."

"Entirely understandable. And that's what kills the fish?"

"Sometimes it kills 'em. Sometimes it does other things. Now you take these college kids"—he pointed to the cars hurrying by—"tomorrow you're going to see them going the other way. And they'll be driving even faster!" He laughed tumultuously, finally bending over to support himself with hands on knees. "*Real* fast!"

"Ha!" said Lee. "How come?"

"How come?"

"Right."

"How come some people don't like cancer? This here is one hell of a lot worse than that."

"The devil you say! How bad is it?"

But the man was not speaking anymore. One of the northbound vehicles had left the highway and stood in need of a mechanic's notice. In any case, Lee was not so certain he really wanted an invitation to stay in this place, so close to old memories. Instead, after availing himself of a soft drink and then wasting another few moments inspecting the family photos on the mantelpiece, a mediocre lot, he returned to the Kaiser and succeeded at last in reentering the stream of southbound traffic.

The further he went, the more the land was turning to outright sand. He zipped past what appeared to be a human rib cage lying by the roadbed, and then shortly after a half-ton javelina vaunting atop one of the dunes. He laughed at it, he who had always been so effortlessly able to separate delusions from the truth. Saw he then a long-hair straggler migrating southward with the help of a staff.

He wanted to stop for the fellow, wanted our man, though it proved a hopeless project in view of the traffic.

He knew that his car was lacking one or more of the half-dozen fluids required, gasoline possibly, or just water perhaps. Edging over into the slow lane, he took three white and one large green pill and washed them down with cigarette smoke. Soon, he'd be able to leave the car altogether and stroll to the beach, it was that near. Until recent years, the clouds had beseemed to him like Confederate generals, and did so still. He drove beneath the somewhat exaggerated chin of one such person and then, in order to stay with the highway, began to tend into a somewhat south-southwesterly direction. The sand in this area was rather dark and never had it actually been as fine and as perfectly disaggregated as tourists had typically been made to believe. In fact, it was lumpy. Accordingly, it was here that Lee left the road and pulled over and got out and began to probe about in a long-ago forsaken motel where, though it were only ten o'clock, a person could pass the night.

The first several rooms were empty, not so the fifth where he intruded upon a little old man sucking on his blanket.

"Pefley," Lee said, extending his hand. "Alabama branch."

But instead of receiving Lee in any sort of fashion, the fellow simply groaned twice and rolled over and pulled the cover over his head. Lee had to shake him.

"Going to Florida," he said, correcting himself almost at once: "All right, I'm there already; I understand that."

The room was disorganized. Among the rubbish Lee saw all manner of stuff, including an accordion and a set of water skis. It gratified Lee that the room did have another bed, although a person would have to relocate a great many incongruous objects, toys mostly, to make it habitable.

"How far, I say how far are we from the Gulf just now?"

Sitting on the edge of his own bed, the man appeared to be afflicted with a headache. Lee gave him more than just a sufficient time before asking again:

"Gulf. How far? I'm talking to you."

"You people. You come down here. This here's the Gulf right here!"

Lee jumped back. "Can't be. Where's the sea gulls and so forth? Snow-white sand?"

"And little children frolicking in the surf?"

"Why yes."

"Okay, I'll show you. If I have to. And then you'll go away?"

He agreed, Lee, to those terms.

Together they marched up and over a brief series of sand dunes and continued on to the edge of the ooze that today looked more like mucilage than ocean water.

"Watch it! Don't get too close to that shit!"

"I see," said Lee calmly. "No swimmers, that's for sure."

"No ships neither. Eats the hell out of their bottoms."

"I dare say." (He bent to gather up what appeared to be a plastic piccolo, a child's toy as he assumed.)

"Throw it back. Not worth two cents at the recycling center."

The sun was high, making it all the harder to discriminate between the detritus and the "sand." A pelican had washed ashore, its ladle-like beak stuffed with matter. Lee then perceived a hypodermic needle (broken) and as many as three or four unscrolled prophylactics lying at hazard. He knew he was in America when he came to a men's bathing suit as big around as a five-ton barrel. With one foot, he turned over half a dozen liquor bottles, expecting to find someone's testament scrolled inside.

"Look for wrist watches!" his colleague called. "And science stuff. Shit, I can fix most nearly everything."

"How long," Lee asked, "have you actually been living in that deserted building?"

"Deserted? You say I been living there, and then you say it's deserted?"

He saw then, Lee, his first electronic device, a ten-inch vibrator with a feather on the nose. "How much for this?"

"Hm? I'll take that."

Lee gave it over. This "Gulf," if truly that's what it was, extended on out of sight for as far as a person's eyesight allowed. He saw claws sticking up out of the ground, and the ruins of a jellyfish formed into a puddle. "All I wanted," he said, "was to gaze one last time upon my remembered Gulf. Look at it now."

"Ah, shut up. By God, that makes my dandruff rise, people like you. Feeling bad about things. All the time!"

"An old man like me. Just *one last gaze.* Only a little bit of solace, that's all I wanted. Memories of what the world used to be."

"Yeah? Well, maybe *you're* the one what's deteriorated."

"I know that! Or possibly, everything's deteriorated at the same pace."

"That'll work. Hey! ain't that a golf club sticking up over there?"

They raced for it. The thing was of metal and might be worth something at the Iron and Steel Exchange.

They scanned the beach till sundown and then tiptoed past the motel receptionist waiting with unending patience for a paying customer to come along. Rather than pass the night with the scavenger, Lee had selected the "honeymoon" suite, so-called, with its mirrored ceiling and black silk sheets. One arrived at the actual mattress by way of a brief staircase of about fourteen inches in elevation. And seldom had he seen so gorgeous a bedspread, a green and lavender entity with whorls on it and illustrations of cut-away seashells exposing the most interesting complexity. He looked forward to spending a few hours beneath such a museum piece, as really it was.

Fourteen

Right away, he fell into a high-quality sleep in which he imagined himself of such small size that he could run unhindered among the whorls and other complexities of that extraordinary quilt. For example, he might leap from one color to another, or clamber to the top of certain elevations in the knap, imperfections of the blanket makers' art. Small as he was, he still remained larger by far than the various life forms, rotifers and such like, competing for territory in so rugged a terrain.

But then, to his regret, he awoke at just past two in the morning and, carrying the blanket with him, reassigned himself to the last cell of the eastern wing of that motel where the traffic noises were somewhat attenuated. Moving carefully, he slinked past the registrar watching television in the central office, an adolescent Hindu singing the high notes of a strange, far-away song that must have related to him in some way.

He slept poorly, slept Lee, for the remainder of that night, then arose very early and packed and peed and was aiming for his automobile when the scavenger came up out of the dark and grabbed him by the shoulder.

"You ain't leaving?"

"I'd like to."

"Hell with that! I got me this ole buddy, and now he's done gone and run his boat up on a sandbar!"

"Ha! How old is he actually?"

"Naw, that's just the way we talk down here. He's not anyway near as old as you."

"Oh? And how old are you exactly? I've been wondering about that."

"Me, too. I'm younger than you, too."

"Possibly. But you're still rather old. Admit it."

"Tell you what, you live down here on the "Silver Coast"—that's what we call it, Silver Coast—and you get old real fast. *Heat rays*, that's what does it."

"Big rays and small."

"Right. 'Course now it's the small ones that's worse. Everybody thinks it's the big ones, but . . ."

"But they're wrong."

"They sure as hell are. Shit, I'll stand out there in them big ones all day long, if I have to."

"And why not, after all?"

"I wipe my ass with 'em!"

"Good man!" said Lee, striving to undo the man's surprisingly strong grip. He recognized that he was being led inexorably in the direction of the ruined beach where, indeed, a vessel of trivial size had run aground on the offshore sandbar referenced above. In theory, Lee was to attach the boat to a twelve-ply cable (supplied by the boat's captain) and drag it to deeper water by means of his antique automobile. Lee demurred.

"No, no. Ha! But I do appreciate the compliment. This old car of mine? Nor do I have gasoline."

The boat captain raised his hand. "I got gas. Lots."

"He does," said the beachcomber. "I've seen it."

"No, the most likely thing is I'd get all bogged down in the sand. You wouldn't want that."

"You call that sand?"

"You get bogged down, I'll pull you out with my old Queen Mary III," the captain said, pointing proudly at the boat.

"I reckon not."

"Look 'buddy,' you're either *with* us and a good person, or you're *against* us. So, what's it's going to be?"

Lee didn't like his tone. Gathering himself up to full height, he put on something of a sneer and spoke out loud and clear: "With you."

In the event, it required him a good deal of backing and filling before he could properly position his worn-out car. Next, rolling his pin-stripe trousers as high as he could, he waded out through the loathsome muck (a mixture of offal and suntan lotion as now he identified it) and tethered the dinghy to the cord. By this time the sun had begun to rise, enabling the dozen or so spectators to see more clearly what the old man was doing.

"Bravo!" said one.

"Damn fool."

He doubted he had as much as a thimble-full of gasoline still remaining to him; even so, Lee used it now, astonished to see how easily the project was accomplished. For the first time in sixty years, he heard cheers directed in his direction. He waved to the people in his insouciant way and was about to ride off into the sunrise when the sea captain stopped him.

"You can't leave now, for God's sakes."

"How come?"

"Well! Who's going to cut the bait and whatall? And do the steering?"

"But I don't have any experience in that line."

"What kind of experience *do* you got? Huh?"

"Well, mostly I've just been thinking. These last years anyway."

"Thinkin'!"

"So you don't have to."

The man raised his arm, but opted not to use it after all.

It wasn't self-evident how the three men could all get on board at the same time, for which reason they did it one by one. Lee saw no conspicuous leaks in the hull, and for a moment it almost seemed to him that this venture might proceed without . . . "*mishap,*" he had started to say, changing that word at the last moment to "catastrophe."

His car meanwhile appeared to be sinking ever so slowly into the grey-green material that ran along the shore for as far as a person could see.

He did not know where they were going, nor why, nor when they might get back. It is true that boat had an engine on it, a twenty-horsepower Evinrude capable of making unexpected good progress through the material. Forming a megaphone with his two hands, Lee yelled to the captain in the bow: "I don't know; somehow I just don't like to think of Aphrodite emerging out of a milieu like this." (He snorted at the thought.) "Do you?"

"What?"

"Aphrodite."

"You bet."

The coast here was rocky and had a blistered look. He was vouchsafed a hasty glance at what appeared to be an archeological site—some two score of mud huts with children running about. Lee smiled and called to them, receiving in return an obscene gesture from one of the girls. But meanwhile, the boat was running *away* from shore, and Lee had hopes of putting all such children out of sight.

It turned out better than he knew. Running at low speed at about a quarter mile from shore they suddenly hit upon an area that was so clear they could see to the bottom of the ocean, some sixteen inches below them. This was about what he had remembered from his youth, a Florida of blue waters with things living in them. Already, the scavenger had lowered his bait and was waiting with an alert expression for a creature to come along and commit one last fatal error. That was when the captain called from the bow:

"Bait your hook Leburt! They's fish down there!"

And did so, choosing for that purpose a red and white lure familiar to him from his experiences. Would only he had brought his grandfather's tackle box! For in a case like that, he doubted not but that he would already have caught all manner of thing. True, he was still being bothered on a regular basis by the *Parsifal* theme, for him a recurring problem since 1974. It tended, that music, to erupt upon him at the most unexpected times. Like this time, to take but one example. In the distance, he could also see clouds drifting at whim, an ocean liner with middle class tourists waltzing on deck, and, along with other things, an ordinary gull flying determinedly into the sun. But perhaps he was only hallucinating once again.

He was not hallucinating, not even when the scavenger just then hoisted a trout of some kind and pinned it to the floor with his boot. This trip had *not* been in vain. Coming nearer, Lee attested that the creature was almost entirely normal, its scales and fins basically intact. His optimism (Lee's) put on new growth. Apart from some four or five deficiencies, the ocean, too, was what it should be, which is to say blue in some places and green in others, and deeper and deeper as one went further and further from shore. But he had been wrong about tourists dancing on board an ocean liner.

It wasn't until almost ten o'clock that he hooked a fish of his own. He was quite calm. Bringing it successfully on board, he was about to free the hook when suddenly he leapt back in dismay, horrified that the thing was possessed of an all-too-human face with long lashes and glittering eyes.

"Jesus!" one of the men shouted out. "Get rid of that thing!"

"No, we certainly don't need this," said Lee. He knew of course the story of evolution, and how natural processes were very often accelerated during times of uncommon stress. Nor were things much better back on land. But that was nothing compared to the horror they all felt when the animal began to make speech-like noises with its mouth.

"Oh, Lord!"

"Get rid of it! I told you once already!"

Lee did try. It had in the meantime begun to rain very slightly, a mere drizzle, milk-colored, with a granular character. His wound was hurting, he hadn't had the sleep he needed, and his wife was waiting in absolute isolation for his promised return. Further, he was an old man, his watch was inaccurate, he had a boil in his nose, and he hadn't had a true meal in how many days. Having suffered from diphtheria when he was young, he waited with dread for its return. And in short, he had experienced just one good thing in his whole life.

For a long time now, he had been thinking of opening her transparent "casket" and changing her over into the red skirt and white sweater of their original encounter. Or rather, what he wanted really was to crawl inside that large and crystalline coffin, and then draw the lid and lock it tight! Instead, that was when the rain began to fall.

"Raining," the captain said. He was an annoying sort of person afflicted with a goiter that looked like a scrotum. And as if that weren't enough, the deformity had warts on it. Appalled by it, and by the ying/yang symbol branded on his forehead, Lee stared at the poor man.

"Hey!" said the fellow. "Don't be looking at that."

"Which?"

"Ear!"

In truth, his ear, too, was bad. Bending to his work, Lee was able to bail out a quart or more of "water" every few seconds, thanks to the bottle of 4% serotonin solution that he had had to empty into the sea. The scavenger went on fishing. The engine went on working. The rain kept on doing what it did, too.

"Do you have insurance?" Lee asked, bailing betimes. (He was staring [inadvertently] at the captain's "scrotum," which seemed to be "breathing" on its own.)

The scavenger kept on fishing. But for the rain, the coast might still have been visible. Lee held to this theory even after he had ignorantly dropped the bottle overboard and was reduced to bailing with his hands. It seemed to him sometimes that the water was rising higher in the boat, sometimes lower, and sometimes he tried not to let it seem like anything at all.

"Ah, me," he said. "And so now this. The least little bit of luck and I could be dead already, yea and dry. Or in my well-built home and reading by the fire!"

Fire? Fact was, he could see at least one place where in spite of the drizzle a considerable blaze had broken out on shore. He saw individuals who looked like stick figures jumping up and down. It was then that the last five minutes of Mahler's Eighth came on in his head. Lee grinned. For insanity, bringing beauty in its train, had continued to be good for him.

By three, the rain began blowing from the east, pushing the skiff continually nearer to what either was an extension of the shore or else a paltry little island with a structure on it. Lee voted for shore *and* structure but had to settle for the last-mentioned only. Later on, he was to remember how they navigated to harbor and pulled the vessel to shore where he remarked some dozen little twenty-four-inch-tall figurines gazing out to sea with lugubrious faces reminiscent of those much more famous ones on Easter Island off the coast of Chile. But which island had been simulating which?

Regarding this "structure," it was a wood frame dwelling that likely had been put up a full seventy or eighty years ago. The porch was hung with pots holding dead flowers, an old-fashioned loom and spindle (for touristic purposes), and a rocking chair nailed to the floor. He peered through the window, Lee, but then leapt back in huge embarrassment when he discovered someone else peering out.

"G'morning!" Lee called, his voice too loud. "Afternoon,

I mean. Seems like we got caught in the rain, ha, ha, and we're looking for a place where we could, you know, like . . ." His voice petered out. In any case, it ought to be obvious what they wanted.

The other person's face had abandoned the window. Inside that building, Lee could see an upright piano, table and chairs, and—he almost fainted—a floor-to-ceiling bookcase with overloaded shelves. Using his binoculars, he was actually able to decipher some of the titles, several of them in foreign languages.

"Good Lord!" he said, getting on his knees and speaking through the mail slot. "Bulgarian? And what other tongues?"

He had to wait for an answer.

"Serbo-Croatian. But I have to use a dictionary of course. Why are you wearing a suit?"

"Me, I was good at Greek at one time. Not so much anymore. But I'm studying German."

"German? I don't even count that one. French, German, those sorts of things."

For the first time in six days, Lee felt ashamed of himself. "My wife knew some Russian."

"Good."

"May we come in?"

"I was reading some Russian last week. Turned out to be Ukrainian."

They both laughed long and hard.

"We can pay," Lee added. "Bed, coffee, change of clothes. What do you think?"

"I have a barometer," said the householder also now getting down on his knees in order the better to be heard by way of the mail slot. His dental condition was mediocre at best, and he had a coating on his tongue, as Lee unavoidably perceived. "That old barometer! It tells me what to expect."

"We don't have one."

"And that individual fishing off my dock—is he one of you?"

"He'd like to get dry, too, I believe. Naw, he won't hurt you."

"Very well." And then, turning to look at the captain: "What is that? Great day in the morning! A goiter?"

"Right. But his ear is in real good shape."

"The size of it!"

"And if I don't have enough cash, why I'll just write you a check," promised Lee.

"Check. We don't have any great number of places here where to cash it you understand. How big a check is it?"

"Not too big. Or, I could give you a hundred dollars in cash I suppose." But Lee hadn't even completed that statement before he saw the little metal flap closing in front of his face. "Okay, two hundred. A hundred for each of us."

"And the fellow with the pole?"

"Okay, three hundred."

"No, I don't think so. I need two hundred for you alone. You're going to be a lot of trouble. I can always tell."

They agreed on that number—four hundred dollars of post-bellum currency bearing the portraits of Civil War criminals. One-by-one, Lee pushed the money through the slot and waited for the receipt that never came. Both men struggled—and it was this that told Lee that his host was probably as old as himself—struggled to their feet. The world waited as slowly, very slowly, the door came open, exposing to the world's view a capacious room with exposed beams and a goodly fire composed seemingly of driftwood. At once Lee went to warm his hands. He had never met a man of his own age whom he couldn't defeat in a fight, or exchange of insults, or a refereed foot race indeed.

"I'm going to take off my shoes and hang my socks up to dry."

"*I* would."

"And then I'm going to look at your books."

"No harm in that. But don't disorganize them please."

Lee had to laugh. "Disorganize a coherent book collection? Not bloody likely. Oh yes, I might make a few *enhancements,* if you will. Using the Dewey system."

"I should have asked for another hundred or two."

Came then a cup of coffee—he assumed it was coffee—delivered by a serious-looking woman in sandals and clothing. Having swallowed his drink, Lee made two steps in her direction, focusing upon a teeny little imperfection on her neck that, as he drew continually nearer, turned out to be a complicated fractal that replicated her whole person in miniature. He put on his glasses and looked at it. Flabbergasted, he took the second cup over into his trembling hands.

"Your wife?"

"She was. We're divorced now."

"Divorced? But my God, man, she looks all right to me!"

"Tax problems."

"Ah." (The woman turned to leave, revealing that her buttocks were about as identical as any two things very well could be.) "Divorced, you say. But don't you realize . . . ?"

"Please! Let us hear no more on that subject."

"And see how she moves!"

They waited for her to get out of view. Lee's associates, crude individuals, already were becoming impatient with these discussions, so much so that Lee began to fear they might take matters and the woman into their own hands. He hastened to appease them.

"The best thing," he said, addressing the host, "would be for you to let us dry ourselves by the fire. Next best, would be a plate of vittles and additional hot coffee for my friends."

"Very well. But then they have to leave."

"They understand that I'm sure." Lee bent closer, whispering to the host: "Besides, they've been plotting against me from the start!"

"What sort of plot?"

"God wot."

"Or God wot not.

"God wot not what."

"God wot not what plot."

They laughed at one another from a distance of about two and a half feet. Lee was beginning to like this person. Generally, he judged a man by his books, and on this showing the fellow was as much as fifty or sixty per-cent as self-educated as himself. Unfair, it seemed, that one of his eyes had been amputated, it's place taken by a yellow agate of exaggerated size.

Night was drawing on, bringing a dense grey fog that while not the very best that he had seen, ranked at a "seven" or even an "eight" on his ten-scale. Things like this, and the sight of a traditional woman busying herself in the kitchen, had almost made the past few hours endurably good. And then, too, there were those dark books, leather-bound, some of them, standing shoulder to shoulder in the wooden bookcase where also an extraordinary seashell was on view.

He migrated toward the books and after giving his adieu to his two coarse colleagues and closing the door behind them, began actually to pluck out some of the volumes and open them up. His opinion improved still further when he saw that his host possessed a very rare boxed set of *Tito Perdue*, a limited printing worth infinitely more than the rest of the collection added up together.

"By golly," he said, "how on earth did you get this!"

"Black market."

"Ah. Must have cost a fortune."

"You can't imagine. I don't even want to talk about it."

"And all these engravings by -------------! And marbled end papers!"

"Yes, and gold dust on the fore edges."

"Rubricated initials! Why, I haven't seen that since I was given a two-hour pass to The University of Texas Rare Books Division."

"And where, pray, do you think I got that copy?"

"Oh, dear."

"Yes. I count upon your discretion."

"Agreed."

They shook solemnly, each man gazing deeply into the other for the assumed underlying aesthetic awareness. He had come to the right place, had Lee, and now he was ready for another cup of coffee. Required by her husband to make an appearance every few minutes, the woman had gotten into pajamas and robe and a pair of slippers that formed a spiral at the toe, like unto those worn by court jesters in old times. Adorable she was, and knew it, and Lee knew it, too, and so did her one-time husband. She was allowed a minute or two to walk up and down, till the men began visibly to tire of it.

"And her, got her at The University of Texas, too?"

"What? Ha! No, no, I found her at . . ." (His voice petered out. He was a pale sort of chap, and looked to be in poor health, the result Lee supposed of too much reading joined to the exigencies of divorce. The fellow also had a Pictish urn of considerable size which however proved empty once the man had left the room. In addition, Lee was cognizant of sea birds and fog horns calling from far and near. He believed he could also hear the ocean's roar as it came to shore at the badly-eroded *Edge of the World*, the fanciful name given to a minor town situated not so far away.

"I'm afraid that I've left most of my luggage in my car," Lee admitted. "And so, I especially appreciate your loaning me this suit." (In fact, it was by no means a superior fabric, and was lacking the double-hemmed satin lining he normally required.) "This seems to be a well-built cottage," he went on, "and quite capable of standing up to the weather." (In fact, the domicile had many deleterious aspects which he now listed, not out loud of course, but mentally at any rate.) "But instead of two by fours, I plan to use four by sixes when it comes time for *my* next home."

"Congratulations."

"What time you have?"

"'Bout midnight."

His intellectual appetite sated, Lee lacked only to be led to bed, preferably by candlelight and with either rum or brandy. And yet, he still had to get undressed, wash face, brush teeth, etc., etc. There seemed no end to these pestilential little obligations that someday would drive him fully insane.

Fifteen

He woke much earlier than usual and inspected the room in the eleven o'clock light. Fond of antiques, the couple actually had a spittoon in the corner wherein a mouse had built a hideaway of her own. Lee stuck his finger in there, but the mouse had gone. Books? There was perhaps a dozen of them arranged, or rather not arranged, in higgledy-piggledy fashion on the windowsill. He read half a paragraph in a modern mainstream novel and then made his way as quickly as he could to the toilet. He had more fain read the instructions on the medicines, a diverting literature pertaining to rheumatism, cramps, nerves, neurasthenia, and several other grieves that had found a home in this place.

His taste this morning was screwed up for waffles or even pancakes, but after a full half-hour had come and gone and nothing of that sort (nor even coffee) had been brought him, he prized open the weighty leather-bound volume that had spent the night with him and began in his amateurish French to read of developments in the legal history of eighteenth-century Burgundy. It was good stuff, pretty good, and had the effect of casting Leland back into those brave days when the French alphabet varied just a little bit from modern practice. But far better than any of this were the woodcut illustrations showing some of the juridical personalities of the day. These were all dead men by now, and yet their features had been saved forever on this rather coarse-grained paper. Coming nearer, Lee thought he could detect a painful smile on the part of a distressed-looking individual dressed in a peculiar hat. Very obviously he was troubled by something, but after two hundred years Lee could not with any confidence pinpoint the nature of the problem.

Life is strange. Going to the window, he witnessed an acre of clear blue water between two oil derricks where the pollution (for his benefit alone?) had momentarily parted. There, in his neurosis, he thought he saw old Triton blow his wreathèd horn. No, actually he had slumbered off to sleep again and hadn't even gotten out of bed as yet.

He needed seventeen minutes to dress himself, and even then he hadn't put on his second shoe. Confident that he *would* now be able to finish, he lay back and gathered his energy. Twenty minutes later saw him coming downstairs in borrowed clothes, his arms outstretched for coffee. He found it flattering that the couple had been waiting for him.

"I thought we might go out a ways and troll for flounders," Lee said. "Those things can be real tasty, if prepared the right way."

The couple looked at each other. Or more properly, each person looked at the other and the other did the same.

"Or speckled trout. I'm not fussy."

"Actually, we already have plans for today."

"Good." He sat. The coffee was better than yesterday's, and the grinds, when he got that far, were of a rich brown coloration. "I'm always ready to listen to your plans. Like I say, I'm not fussy about things like that."

"Actually, I need to go to town, visit my sister," the man said, looking down into his cereal. "She's in poor health, you understand."

"Ah. Hey! We'll take her trolling with us."

"Don't have a boat."

"Sure, you do! How else could you visit your sister? And all this time"—he chuckled politely—"I thought *my* memory was bad!"

The trolling brought little success, nor had the man's sister come with them. They caught naught but catfish, a doleful species full of evil fins. Using the paddle, they *were* able to fend off most of the "goobergs" (to use the vernacular) that came their way, including most notably a foot-thick coagulation carrying a sealed jar with a fetus in it.

"Not that I'm opposed to abortion," explained Lee once they had returned to the comfort of the well-built house. "Heck, if I had my way, it'd be mandatory for most people."

They gasped.

"Gasp! Never thought I'd actually hear anybody say that. I do hope you'll stay with us a few weeks, we have so much to talk about."

"Stay? That's an unusual attitude I must say."

"And that will give us a chance to show you our little island."

"It *is* small certainly. By the way, you don't have any more coffee, do you? And that toast with the real good jelly?"

It was admittedly a warm and comfortable and fairly

well-built cottage with a view that in pre-pollution days might have taken a person's breath away. Books, toast, a radio antenna, and that upstairs mattress that retained Lee's poor silhouette. There was food in the pantry (he divined) and in an outside pen some half-dozen boxer dogs trained to ward away the immigrants, an impudent people wont to transit here on their way to Tallahassee and points even further than that. Chicago, for example.

"I wouldn't care to irritate those dogs of yours," Lee said, speaking too softly for the creatures to hear him. "Whew! They could rip a person into pieces I suppose."

"Them? They're boxers. Mostly they just wait there night after night, hoping for a chance to play with the illegals. Worthless. What, you want 'em?"

Lee jumped back. "All right."

The island *was* small, a mere ten or fifteen acres with, however, a rocky elevation that let the owners evade the high waters that historically had done so much damage to the coastal area. Indeed, they had worn a pathway to the summit where the view must have been superb at one time. From this elevation they could observe the whales, their great corpses floating upside down. Observe they also could some of the seaweed "rafts" used by migrating Hondurans and their Federal escorts.

"They excrete on the beach."

"Yes, and we had one case where a tourist had drowned and they took turns enjoying themselves on her body. Wonderful people. Soon to be the majority."

"Hey! Careful what you say. They've got laws about that."

Maintaining silence, they continued their exploration. At some remote date, a Roman ship had gone down in this area, a terrible accident that still sometimes yielded flagons of old wine for the enjoyment of this and neighboring islands. Earlier still, an enormous undersea volcano had created the state of Florida. And at one time the world itself had been a hot molten sphere like the sun.

"I *would* like to stay a few days," Lee allowed. "But then I'll need to get back to my wife."

"Wife?"

"Yes. She waits for me in a cube of plastic ice. No, go ahead and laugh if you wish."

The woman snickered, but there was no real mirth in either of them, not till the man turned him around, looked him in the face and began a blatant outright laughter that continued for a time.

"Suspended animation I suppose? Very good! Sir, let me tell you something true: You are by far *the very oddest guest* we've ever had out here."

Lee waved it off modestly. In his youth, he had spent a good deal of time trying *not* to be odd but had finally given up on it at a certain age of sixty.

By 2:15, they had rounded the bend and were able to view the feces and campfires left by Latin Americans fleeing the results of their behavior back home. Shielding his eyes, Lee saw that DeFuniak Springs, a once-lovely town famous for its honey, was burning slowly in the distance.

"No, that's just the paper mill," said his host.

"Quite an imagination, yours," the woman added.

"Yes? Well like you said, I'm odd."

"Certainly, you're odd. As is everyone over the age of sixty. Tell me, Leford, do you like this world? The way it is? Compared to how it was?"

"Hate it. And had the founders seen what it would come to, I do believe they'd have renewed their allegiance to the king."

"Us, too, Lee. And so, we're going to leave it."

Lee looked at them individually and collectively and jumped back. "Now, when you say 'leave it,' I don't suppose you . . . Naw!"

"Oh yes, and soon."

"I had the prettiest daughter, Lee. She's with a rock group now."

"Jesus."

"I did try, Lee, I really did. Wasted eight months as Adjunct Professor of Consilium Studies at the Brent Campus of Centreville University where I was coerced into the "Bleetonian Theorem," so-called. It was that or loss of tenure. And in all that time, I never made ten percent of the salary of the school's Deputy Assistant Strong Side Tackle Coach, Emeritus."

"Bleet . . . ?

"Post-patriarchal synthesis of neo-gestalt parapsychology and metachemistry. An ingenious piece of shit set up by a squad of English professors."

"No tenure for you then, yes?"

"Certainly not! They said I was a latent racist. I ask you; do I really look like that sort of person?"

"Racist?"

"No, latent."

"You're asking me? I don't even know the difference between latent fingerprints and real ones."

"And then my two sons. So far as I can tell, they spend most of their time promoting Bleetonianism from their printing press in the Catskills."

"Good gracious. Three children altogether?"

"Four. But Timothy—he was the promising one—died last year of bad circulation. Seems he had gotten involved with some sort of progressive bondage group."

"Strange fate for a country that might almost . . ."

". . . might almost have been like Greece? Yes, I've heard that formula from you at least twice already."

"Up till last year, there'd been no divorces in *my* family for two hundred years."

"Maybe so. But *my* uncle used to farm fifty acres of strawberries without machinery."

They had come to the end of the island. But because

the conversation was as interesting as it was, they turned and came back again. Said the host:

"At this very moment, Lee, a couple is sitting down in Los Angeles to a five-hundred-dollar meal of pâté and hummingbird tongue. In another country far away, a man waits in an interrogation center to have his eyes gouged out. See any causal connection between those procedures."

"The nature of things."

"And that's why we're leaving."

Lee had no answer to that point of view. They were facing ancient Europe but, owing to the girth of Florida, could see nothing of it.

"And yet, even here on native ground," Lee inserted, "we've had our Edgar Poe and John Wilkes Booth. No, I think I'll stay around for a while."

"But Lee. Maybe it's not the country that's gone bad, but me and you."

"I've considered that."

"But rejected it?"

"Hmm."

They supped gingerly that night on what remained of the shrimp and then drifted out to the porch to debate about matters. Abetted by biotechnological advances, the little black flies had become three times their size. Lee killed one, his host and hostess four. Thunder in the west where soon rain would continue staining the Gulf. Picking up at about where he had left off, the host began grumbling about an assortment of things.

"They all look alike nowadays," he said, "and are held together by glue."

"Books?"

"I wanted a copy of Caedmon, but do you think they had it? Hell no."

"Yes, but he wasn't a woman and never lived in New

York. What did you expect?"

"And Priscian's grammar. The lady hadn't even heard of him."

"Your special period I presume?"

(He had been served, Lee had, with a beverage that he rather liked, an amber-colored affair with a virtual cherry in it. Having quaffed down a full measure of the stuff, he held out his empty tumbler where the woman couldn't fail to notice it.)

"I see it," she said.

Suddenly, the host came to his feet and, three-fourths drunk already, pointed off to a wan light flickering weakly in the extreme East.

"There they are! Boat load of common Mestizos from Mexico!"

They hurried. Never before had Lee so regretted his absent revolver now rusting in his old Kaiser car. They had perhaps twenty minutes and no more before the Coastguard would have disembarked these thirty or fifty or perhaps hundred low-wage workers onto some part of their little island. Lacking firearms, Lee ran to the dogs and pointed them to the danger. They wanted to play.

"No, no, no," he pleaded. "What's the matter with your breed? By God, you *look* ferocious enough." In fact, three of the dogs were grinning and the fourth was asleep. Even so, Lee linked them together with their heavy-duty leash and dragged them down to shore where all at once the whole mob of them began chasing after a small white crab.

The host had a flashlight whereas the woman had brought what looked very like a factual shotgun that was nearly—it *was* a shotgun!—nearly as long as Leland's grandfather's. Lee counted five (not a hundred) trespassers wading ashore with the sort of relaxed insouciance that seemed to say the country belonged to *them* already and no longer *us*.

"Miscreants!" he yelled, trying at the same time to cope with the ecstatic dogs presently striving to divide between them a small white crab. Running forward at poor speed, Lee identified three Mexican types and (and here he almost fainted) a verifiable Guatemalan naked above the waist. But where, pray, was his .357 when most it was needed? "In the car!" he said, having already responded to that query just a short time earlier. That was when he fell and rolled, covered head to foot by four frolicking dogs.

"Goddamn it!" he elaborated. His mouth had sand in it and some appeared to have gotten into his eye as well. But where were his glasses? By hap, he had fallen in such a way that the reeking waves could reach him. The woman had come up even with him by this time and was going after the trespassers with a better chance of success than he, certainly, had evinced.

"Kill!" he yelled. "The Guatemalan first and the others soon after!"

His glasses: they had been taken by one of the dogs and carried to a remove where he could see one of the lenses scintillating in the moon. He crawled in that direction, conscious that his host had turned back and was trudging sadly homeward. To his astonishment (Lee's), the Mestizos were already setting up their tents and excreting on the beach. Worse, one of the dogs had gone over to the other side.

It was not a good time for Lee. Without glasses, he could distinguish neither the stars nor moon, nor the subhuman transporting a transportable radio on his back. Lee watched as best he could while the man ran up an antenna, seated himself, and then began reporting in gibberish to people on the other side of the world.

It was 500 rods to the cottage, a distance that twice made it necessary for Lee stop and rest. Sinking down on the sofa, he complained at length about the dogs and glasses, his revolver and his car. Finally, he summoned up the effrontery to ask for coffee and two or more of the cinnamon rolls that were so good.

He spent three days without speaking, and the couple did the same. Oh yes, they might see one another along the beach, or quarantined in the "library," or scanning the seascape with Leland's binoculars, they might do that. But mainly, they went their ways, a vacation time for thoughtful people like themselves. Came then the time when the woman climbed the hill and stood there silently for a moment.

"Okay, I get it," said Lee. "I'll pack my things and be out of here by, say, three o'clock."

"No, no; we'd like you to stay. Long as you want."

They were examining a star so bright that it was plainly visible in the daytime sky. Lee pointed to it.

"Yes," she said. "I noticed it yesterday. Never saw a star so bright!"

"Star, madam? No, what you see there is the residue of a super black nova in galaxy NGC1068. Don't you get the Keck Observatory newsletter? They go to a lot of trouble for people like you. And all those Corybantic stars? Pastel dwarves, very common this time of year."

"I had no idea."

And then, in a confessional mode: "It's time, really, when I should pack my bag and give you two some peace."

"I don't think so. We're the ones who're leaving, Matt and me, and you could do us a great favor, if you would."

"'Leaving?' Again, with that?"

"I know you're going to take good care of the dogs, and we have that bird, too. The red one that's always talking?"

"I'm acquainted with him, yes. Couldn't escape him even if I wanted to!" He laughed in friendly fashion. Or snorted rather, but still in a more or less friendly way. Sick to death of that bird, his snort had an edge to it. And yet, she seemed not to notice his implicit underlying feeling.

"You can turn him loose, if you want to. He won't survive of course."

Lee agreed. Off in the distance, he had detected an oil barge emptying itself into one of the clear spots. Spreading over the sea, that enormous stain gave off all the colors of the rainbow, and in proper sequence, too. The woman went on:

"We have the chemicals. Matt wants to play the *Liebestod*, and we'd like you to turn the machine off when it's through."

"Ah? And who will the soprano be?"

"And Matt wants you to have any book you want. All of them, if you can manage."

Lee, his mind now slowly coming to the urgency at hand, turned and looked at her. She'd had no sleep in such a long time, and for the past week had pretty much eschewed *all make-up of any kind*, the first time he had seen that behavior in a woman of never mind what age. Still an alluring woman despite it all, she had a well-arranged face and two bottomless eyes full of absolute filth. Lee had little doubt but that she had engaged in premarital sex at some stage. Even so, he replied politely.

"Leaving, you say."

"Why, yes. Want to come with us? We were watching television this morning and realized the time has come."

"But my God . . . Leaving! Naw, not if you'll be listening to the *Liebestod*. Can't be done! Okay, it can be done. After all—and I'm thinking about it at this very moment—suicide is not nearly so bad as what happens to most people." (Survival with loss of personality.) "Yes, by God, this is going to put you *far ahead* of the generality of people."

But she had already begun to thread her way down the hill, Lee following at a distance. Her ass was still quite good, and if viewed unclothed, wouldn't have been significantly inferior to a nineteen-year-old's.

"When?" he called.

"Three o'clock. And be there please."

Christ, he was dismayed! Or rather somewhat envious and perturbed at the same time as dismayed. Not precisely "envious" so much as afflicted with a sort of involuntary admiration for a decision so bold and understandable and apposite to the times. "No more television!" he said. And: "No more goddamn little electronic devices that go off in the night." That was when the most authentic benefit of all suddenly occurred to his head: "And no more great big cities with debased youths walking back and forth! No more New York!"

He was quite happy. In testimony of that, he lit up his second-to-last cigarette and then gathered up a (broken) seashell and skipped it across the foam. The time was just past noon and very soon his two and only best friends would either be unconscious or rotating head over heels through paradise, denouements equally worth cheering for.

He was still reading at two o'clock, still sometimes gazing out over the ruined sea, still dismayed. But for his determination to lie him down at last inside the chrysalis of his absent wife, he might almost, but not quite, might almost have connected himself to the project that was now just forty-six minutes away. Having finished the chapter, a good one detailing recent findings in ninth-century Northumberland pottery, he arose, adjusted his tie, and brushed the "sand" from his Italian suit that now again was mostly dry. He had intended to stroll the whole circumference of the island and having progressed some thirty feet, decided to continue. The beach had a considerable scum on it, but even so he was able to point out the usual things—a plastic comb, manufactured products, a dime-size button from the Kellogg organization with the picture of Skeezix on it. Save for this latter, he resisted the temptation to collect such objects, preferring instead to cut across the island so as both to abbreviate his course and avoid the human detritus playing volleyball while up to their knees in the surf. It was 2:49.

And now it was 2:50 exactly, time to amble back to the cottage and do what he must. Not that he looked forward to it! On the other hand, there were those books. He saw, he thought, a fire on the mainland, in fact merely the release of a column of odoriferous smoke from one of the coastal suburbs where so many South-despising big city pastrami-eaters had opted to retire.

One last paragraph he read and then, licking his lips over the quality of the prose, entered the cottage. The music was almost finished, nor had they selected his own favorite soprano. Taking up his courage, he nudged open the bedroom door and waited for his eyes to adjust.

Turns out that instead of remaining in an embrace, the woman had repositioned herself at the last moment, allowing her left thigh to be seen. Lee appraised it and turned off the machine. Already, the flies had gathered at seven of the eight corners of the couples' four eyes and were supping on the fluids there to be found. But was not Lee himself being observed from above by the just-departed spirits of his defunct hosts? In any case, he tilted his face upwards and smiled for a few moments. Matt appeared simply to have dropped off into a sleep that was neither uncomfortable especially, nor yet particularly pleasant. Lee jumped back, cognizant of a little gesture, almost certainly involuntary, of the man's index finger. Both persons had let their toes point outward in the "feetle," position, as Lee amusingly called it, proof positive of their real condition. As for the toxin itself, it was simply a white powder held in a laboratory bottle with a glass stopper that itself lay on the floor. So much for this particular experience, which ranked very near the top of Leland's seventy-eight-year career.

They had left three letters, one for himself, one for their only halfway decent son, and one holding a thousand-dollar donation to an extinct organization calling for the protection of a species of Canadian protozoa, now also extinct. Lee never opened the son's letter, though he might, for example, hold it up to the light. Never had he seen so many clichés, so much sentimentality offered up so apologetically. As to the message left for himself, we know nothing of its ultimate dispensation.

Sixteen

Our man spent five further days in that cottage, till he could endure no longer the effusions emanating from the bedroom. Not that he was idle during that time, not with dogs to feed and some 1,524 volumes needing to be collated and appraised, and in some cases needing to be read in whole or in substantial part at least.

By Wednesday, he had located a robust suitcase in adequate condition, a medium-size affair pasted with airline decals from Austria and Hungary and other places of that kind. It seemed to him meet therefore to choose imprints from those same European parts, some sixty-two pounds of them. He focused especially on seventeenth-century material, leather-bound volumes that had failed incunabula status but by a decade or two. He found a two-volume set bound in white pigskin, and although he wouldn't be able to cope with the Latin, made this his second choice out of that whole collection. He found and kept the famous 1809 Dresden edition of Linnaeus, as also a butterfly book with some of the most supreme colored illustrations ever seen. A first edition of

Cuthbert came to light, an early Thomas Browne in good condition, also Burton's *Melancholy* in which a learnèd man had posted a number of emendations in microscopic script. But mostly it was early Europe that had riveted the dead couple's attention, an obsession represented in historical chronicles (naïve, many of them), as also in grammars and glossaries, cartularies and paleographies enough to cause our boy's head to spin. A thousand years might go by, but still he would not have mastered even just eight-tenths of all the world's better books.

The suitcase was not as stalwart as indicated, wherefore he took two white sheets and by reinforcing them back to back with each other and adding a third to form a "bag," or "sack," improperly so-called, proceeded to fill it up with books. It weighed, that bundle, fifty-seven pounds precisely, but would have weighed more had not the suitcase been taken back to the attic. Even so, it was a drastic weight for someone like Lee, or Lee himself actually, who had not recently lifted anything more weighty than a ballpoint pen. Counting up to three, he hefted the thing high and strode about the room with it. He had been playing the best of Bartok's quartets, and that, in combination with the cooling weather, the sound of flotsam impinging on shore, and the occasional immigrant spying through the parlor window, it all gave him the urge to be up and gone and most of the way back to Alabama before the arrival of further transients to this condemned island.

He had almost finished when he stopped and then hastened back to the library to add to his bag a rather quaint and curious volume of seventeenth-century lore. The dogs had fed but with sea water deemed impotable for this species, he irrigated them from the faucet and then herded them down to the cove where the couple's rather pathetic little rowboat had been drawn ashore. Would he, or would he not, be able to launch the thing out to sea? He would, and having escorted it to a decent depth while ruining his shoes for the third time in just two weeks, he returned for the dogs (renamed by him after sub-atomic particles) and stowed them in the bow. It was a fair day, as these things go, and at first he made pretty good progress with the oars. If he wasn't mistaken (but he was, and not for the first time either) a town was burning a mile or two down coast, women jumping from the windows, rainmakers dancing on the heath.

Lee kept on rowing, waiting from moment to moment for the hull to give way and brine come dashing inside to moisten the books. If he had to, probably he could have swum the distance when he was young, but the dogs probably not. "Ah, me," he said. "Here am I, drifting on high seas, and I don't even know why!" Nor could he piece together the last ten days, not with his seventy-eight-year-old mind and the ramifications of that fate. "Last I remember, I was running through the fields of my grandfather's farm." Suddenly, he veered, avoiding a collision with a half-million-dollar vessel under management of a clutch of nugatory youths.

The shore, when he reached it (and even before) was littered with paper cups and beer bottles and penny coins considered by many, but not by Lee, too unimportant to retrieve. He then parked and tried to bring together the four grinning dogs. The suitcase was heavier than he wanted, and meantime he was carrying his spare clothes and shaving equipment in a damp paper bag in peril of dissolution. Treating himself to his last cigarette, he frightened a passing motorist with one of those miniature explosions that this particular tobacco was wont to produce.

He was on a highway that paralleled the Gulf for as far as he could see. He fully expected to lose half his animals before anyone offered them a ride. He had anticipated in advance that a speeding car full of tourists/youths would have something to say, which of course they did. That was when a kind lady—and he had always counted upon the kindness of ladies—ventured across the road and spoke with him.

"Excuse me, but are you waiting for the bus?"

Lee lifted his hat. "Yes, ma'am, we are. Hard, for a person my age."

"Well, of course! How far are you going?"

Lee pointed, and to make an involved story much shorter, it developed that she had a husband, her husband had a car, and the whole group of them were given a ride back to where Lee believed his Fraser was lodged in the sand.)

"So many dogs!" the woman said, once they had fitted themselves into her reputable Swedish car. She had good legs for a woman and a decent face as well. Lee made no mention of these however. Her "husband," on the other hand, looked like a consultant or insurance man, a furniture store owner or something equal to that.

"What are their names?"

"I haven't had them long," said Lee, averting the need to reveal their scientific appellations. "I call this one 'spot.'"

"Oh, how cute!"

About as cute as a dead cigar butt floating in a three-fourths empty cup of cold coffee with ashes drifting in it. "Yes, ma'am."

It needed less than a short time to deliver Lee and the animals to where his old-fashioned car stood looking out to sea, sentinel-like, on the grey bleak shore. He offered to pay for the ride, Lee, and was flabbergasted when the man billed him a dollar for the fuel and six for the labor.

"Seven?" Lee respectfully inquired. "But it can't have been more than half a mile!"

"Want I should take you back?"

A Jew! Lee paid, taking out a full ten-dollar bill, hand-ing it over, and then waiting with more patience than should have been necessary for the two dollars of change. Always, he had depended upon the decency of some people, if not of others. For their own part, the dogs had intuited that the Fraser was theirs and had managed, three of them, to occupy it through the half-open window. Presumptuous creatures, no doubt about that, and but for their hilarious faces, he would have disinherited them as recently as yesterday. "Now I'm going to try and start this car," Lee explained. No one was within a thousand rods of him, and yet, outside that perimeter, the Americans were laughing at him still—such was his mental state at this time.

The car had almost no gasoline, it would be fair to say, and it delighted Lee that it did actually start and did succeed finally in returning to the asphalt highway. He was quite pleased, or for the nonce at least. Less pleased when he saw fumes arising from front and back. The dogs were yelping but could not get out.

He coaxed the car forward for perhaps two hundred yards and then pulled into a service station consecrated to northern tourists. Here, one could buy miniature bales of cotton (about two inches square) wrapped in confederate flags. Or a quart of magnolia honey with a picture of Ty Cobb on it. One could buy postcards showing the Suwannee River under cedars festooned with Spanish Moss. Or, a two-pound bag of stone-ground grits, or pancake syrup, or a framed portrait of Scarlet and Rhett. Seeing all this, Lee hung back in the shadows and counted the purchases being consummated on all sides. As for himself, he invested solely in the grits, a small paper sack of boiled peanuts, and fifteen gallons of their least expensive gasoline.

It was good to be on the highway once again, once again speeding between the historical scenery on both sides, a dual panorama that the historians of the future would have given anything to see. He went past a small goat operation, an extensive enterprise specializing in the dwarfs of the species. He passed a grist mill in a pretty good state of preservation, and then a French chalet parked all around with Japanese cars. There was no doubt but that the South was growing prosperous, a by-product of the deterioration in the quality of its people. And where now, pray, were the gaunt men of yesterday? Gone to fat while watching soccer matches on European television. He wanted to vomit.

Having again filled the car with oil, water, fuel, and windshield wiper fluid, he transited three hours later into the outlying extensions of a major city. It was his opportunity to deviate into what appeared to be a dangerous-looking slum with people standing about. Slowing, he passed two youths in baseball hats and then, slowing further, struggled to get a view of their facial qualities. He saw a fifteen, or possibly a sixteen-year-old negress skiing down the sidewalk. "Skiing," he said, as she wasn't able, seemingly, actually to lift her feet from the pavement. "Pregnant," he said, owing to her condition.

He never said anything to any of them. As for the restoration of slavery, he had never made the least progress in popular opinion and no longer cared to try. And as for "progress," he spit all over that, and all tangential concepts as well.

He knew that his car was out of kilter when his angle of vision began running to the sky. Reluctantly, or angrily rather, he pulled over and after anathematizing the dogs, went into the trunk of the car where the spare tire was not only just flat but had putrefied as well. He cursed. Once an object has been manufactured and purchased, it ought never give trouble again—such was his thinking. Thus Lee, who stood plucking worriedly at his chin, which was to say until he was joined by a young blackamoor of about 150 pounds.

"What you need man?"

Lee smiled. "Tire."

"What else you need?"

"What you got?'

"Got weed."

"Why am I not surprised? And girls?" (The boy wore surgical bandages where his fingerprints used to be—Lee noticed this and wrote it down in memory.)

"No problem, man, *no problema*. You name it."

"You don't have any, say, like twelve-year-olds?"

"Got one that's eleven. She'll do it for you man, no problem."

(Lee reached for his revolver.) "How 'bout like, say, four years old?"

"Say what? You're sick man. Whoa! I don't deal that shit. What, you a cop?"

Lee now allowed the Smith & Wesson to make an appearance just outside his pocket. It discomforted him to see that the boy, except that his was a Sig, had done the same. They looked at each other. Said Lee to himself: "I *cannot* allow Judy's husband to die like this, I just can't." And to the boy: "I cannot allow Judy's husband . . ."

"Better git yo ass on out of here man, or I'm going to splatter your brains all over this shit!"

"Really! Well, let's just call it a stalemate, shall we? Right now, my plan is to git on out of here and just keep on going!"

And did so. Arriving two minutes later at a juncture of state and federal highways, he turned right and kept on going.

But had not traveled a great distance before his conscientious part had overwhelmed his common sense. Again slowing, he passed a grocery store dealing in software and shoe ware and then soon after came to the police station itself, a thirty or forty-story sandstone pile with a life-size bronze of Baby Face Nelson out front. Lee parked and locked the car and, ignoring the amazement of the people relative to his ensemble, bounded up to the massy door of the building and not without effort managed to pull it open.

There was a sacrosanct atmosphere in that place, very like what prevails in post offices and libraries and kindred places; he had seen the same thing on that day in his youth when he had been brought by the police to a headquarters of just this nature. Putting on the self-assurance of confident old age (confident because there wasn't much they could do to a person of his kind), he marched straightway to the official sitting in a high chair at the back of the foyer.

"I want to report something," he said. "Crime."

"Nigger with a Sig Sauer?"

Lee jumped back.

"He's one of ours."

"I see! Now when you say 'one of ours,' are you also saying . . ."

"That's right. Leave him alone, he won't bother you."

"Yeah, but . . ."

"You don't hear so good? Leave him alone, and we'll let you go. No charges."

Lee blinked. One of the dogs had squeezed inside and was struggling to get at the lawman's crotch. Lee summoned the animal and slapped him three times, not too severely, across the snout.

"Got a license for that dog? I doubt it."

"That's exactly where I was going. I was going there just a minute ago, as it were. To get that license."

"Good, good. 'Cause I got me a St. Bernard at home could beat the shit of *that* thing."

"Oh? And could he beat the shit out of *four of them*?"

"You got four?"

"I do."

"That's different. I don't know about four."

"I should think not! I expect just *two* of mine could handle yours. Easy."

"What'd you say?"

"Easy."

"Well now, you're a real hard nose, aren't you? Soon as I saw you, I said (speaking to myself you understand) 'he's not going to give *me* a hard time, not this fellow.' And now we're talking about it, where'd you get that suit? Salvation Army?"

"Listen, I happen to be a *contributor* to the Salvation Army! Always have been."

"And always will?"

"Why yes. Probably."

"Not if you're in jail."

Etc.

He drove to the North, stopping betimes for water and transmission fluid. He preferred to circumvent the towns, no matter the miles it added to his journey homeward to his wife, his canned foods, the home-grown potatoes resting in the cellar, his books and subscriptions, and the good neighbor who lived across the field. Hell, he even missed the crows who gathered afternoons to jeer him out of bed.

Today, the weather was silent and void, offering no resistance to the progress of his car. Ahead were mountains, smoke coming off the summits, and dark pine forests that looked like corduroy. These visions, not to put too fine a point on it, were more admirable by far than mere human beings, a weak species full of stratagems for things that had no worth. Matter of fact, he saw one now, a middle age person talking to himself bitterly behind the wheel of a high-priced car. What did he want? Lee pulled up alongside him and looked wonderingly into his face. Women and more money, or more women and try to be content with the existing money? Or perhaps he wished for elective office, smaller taxes (he could be happy then), free beer, and an end to crabgrass. Televised football games that go on for twenty quarters? Perhaps he knew someone he wanted to slaughter, or someone else he wanted to . . . But at this point Lee gave up talking to himself.

The next town gave no choice but to enter it and push his way slowly down an avenue lined on both sides with dilapidated enterprises. He saw a hardware man in an apron sweeping the sidewalk in front of his unsuccessful business, an encouraging sign to a person like ours who loves those only who are always failing and always trying. He nodded, nodded Lee, to a policeman directing traffic, a portly individual, quite ignorant, who had done more to defend civilization than a thousand New York columnists married to lawyers. Lee obeyed his signals implicitly, coming to a quick halt behind that self-same high-price vehicle mentioned earlier. It interested him when suddenly the trunk of the car popped open to reveal a large canvas bag with something in it.

He turned eastward at the next block, went a distance, and then came to a service station where he was able to get out and endure the laughter directed at his car, the dogs, the parrot, and his own confessedly odd uniform.

"He's got him one of those cars!" said the manager, a man in dark glasses who, as Lee studied him, seemed to have a drain tube hanging out of his cuff.

"Yeah! And look at that bird in there, flying all around. Damn!"

"Them dogs is going to eat that bird."

"Dressed funny, too. Oh, oh, here he comes."

Lee endured it. Waiting for the excitement to die down, he ordered a new tire (expensive) and a refill of the three essential liquids his car required.

"Heh, heh," the manager said (he was chuckling still),

"oil and gas, yes sir." And then: "I guess you must be kind of partial to dogs like that. No, I'm just saying."

"Yes, I suppose I am. New filter too, please."

"Got yourself a red bird, too, seems like. Where'd you pick him up at?"

"Friend of mine."

"Friend give it to you?"

"No, the *bird* is a friend of mine. Sort of."

"You're from up North, right?"

"No, no. Look, I'm just as good an Alabama man as you are! Better maybe."

"This here is Florida. 'Bama's over there." (He pointed.) "Me, I don't go over there much anymore, not since that time I . . ." (His voice faded away.)

He paid all his bills, Lee, and purchased two extra containers of steering fluid. His car was an *alcoholic* of sorts, he said to himself humorously, a remark that reminded him to go into his glove compartment and take out a pint bottle of tequila in which the original worm had given birth before she died. Lee was but a short ride from Alabama and was unwilling to exclaustrate the bird until they were well within the state. The dogs had meanwhile all fallen off to sleep and, in the mirror, looked like a discard of legs, tails, and muzzles that had been tossed in at random. All his life, Lee had wished for some higher species to come onto the stage of the world. This wasn't them.

Night was coming on, inspiring Lee to take out his miniature binoculars and avail himself of the dying light. He noticed a video rental doing good business just next to a seafood restaurant specializing in the armadillo fad. But mostly his attention was for his oil and fuel, his bright red bird, and the dogs that were beginning to come awake. Water for the dogs, seed for the bird, oil for the car, and for him . . .

He stopped at the first restaurant that came into ken,

a noisy place with a good many young people in it. Further down the road (and far more to his liking) was a sodden little café in which some half score of truck drivers and retired people sat hunched silently over their oats and whey. Lee entered, posed in the doorway (no one laughed), and went direct to the remotest alcove still available. Taking out his glasses, he critiqued the portrait of a certain famous football coach posted above the cash register. He turned then to the man in the next booth, a depressed individual with a beard that had recently been soaking, it seemed clear, in his tankard of yellow beer. For a long time, this person simply stared at Lee, before then speaking up loud and clear:

"So, you figure you're better than us, is that what it is?"

Lee stared back just as simply. "Wouldn't care to go on living otherwise."

To his credit, the fellow laughed. Lee made room for the man's beer and platter and unspeakable cigar. Face to face they sat, two old men with a great many overlapping years of too much experience continued too long. Lee waited for his story, which came in a rush before half a minute had gone by.

". . . whore, more or less. I tried to be the right kind of parent but, you know . . ."

"Don't blame yourself. The best parents in the world can't stand up against this." (He indicated the world with the hand that bore his fifty-four-year-old band of gold.) "Did she remarry?"

"Twice. Going on three."

"Good. And meanwhile, she's living with a roofer, or welder, someone who looks like you."

"Hey, you're pretty good at this! Sorry about what I said."

Allowing himself time for the compliment to soak in, Lee lifted his own beer and drank. "Well sir," he picked up, "I recommend you start a diary. *Materials for The Use of All Future Historians*, I suggest you call it." And then, muttering only to himself: "They still won't believe it however."

Across the aisle, he then noticed a handsome Caucasian female dining cheerfully with a member of the opposite race. The girl might have been an Isolde, an Héloïse, an Andromache, while as for the boy, he looked like a Devonian restroom attendant. Forcing himself to look away, Lee's gaze next ran up against a fat woman with a gorgeous blue and yellow tattoo offering a portrait of herself in congress with an alligator. It was one of his weaknesses, Lee's, that he sometimes allowed himself to imagine that he was speaking with an advanced person, or coadjutor as it were. With that in mind, he bent forward and revealed to the man one of his more unverifiable beliefs:

"No, it's beauty alone that matters, beauty which, like time and space, would be just as wonderful had people never existed."

"I told you I was sorry! Anyway, I got to go now."

Lee allowed him to do so. He had put himself in a place whence he could see lights burning in the upper stories of the tall buildings across the way. But what actually were they *doing* there? Devising advertising slogans? Mutual funds? Public relations? Post-doctoral courses on tax minimization? Modern men adding rows of figures while moving papers about? "Better they had been mule skinners, ships' captains, navigators, stone masons, horse wranglers, almoners, prospectors, or indigo farmers instead of meekly following in the patterns laid down by their third-rate fathers," as he revealed out loud. Finally, he just came out with it: "Better to lie in the grass and blow the stars about."

He took up the menu, put it away in his satchel for purposes of research, and then took two white pills and a swig of calomel. At this moment, he had a sty in his eye, a boil in his nose, and other discomforts as well. Old age! And was there indeed to be no exemption for people who had read 10,000 books? Reluctant to leave the warmth and good smells of the café, he dawdled over a wedge of pie with a slice of cheese on it. He then endured a few minutes of television where an experiment in social engineering was going on, a comedy designed to accustom people to the fade-out of the Caucasian element. It portrayed, and with great subtlety, a handsome black polo player being served a cocktail by a defeated-looking white male in a dress.

"Hmm," he said. "This was scripted, if that's the word, by someone in New York." In any case, it drove him to the cashier where, using some of his grandfather's coins, he paid for himself and for a sad-looking policeman sitting alone in alcove far away.

"Oh, I just love those old retro outfits!" the woman said sincerely.

Seventeen

He drove slowly out of town, muttering to the sidewalk people who should have been in bed by now. He heard the sound of a whiskey bottle exploding on the pavement, or brandy possibly. Lee drew his revolver and cuddled it in his lap. These people could have mastered the Japanese writing system in the time they gave to drifting back and forth in shopping malls. Not that the Japanese "system" made great sense when a phonetic arrangement would have sufficed quite as well.

Or better really. Thinking of it, he passed slowly in front of a ten-acre grid of tennis and basketball courts, an expensive installation pursuant to a taxpayer demand for an alternative to criminal activity. He came to a twinkling movie theatre where a new production of *The Scar-*

let Letter was showing, a daring and boundary-breaking version showing full penetration. He turned to observe a spate of ovulating girls in earrings and skirts. He did sometimes feel bad about these people, a restless population condemned forever to an unavailing search for something better. But mostly he did not.

He woke at a little past eleven, startled to find the car positioned at an angle in the roadside ditch. Five minutes he sat there, rifling back over his recent memories in an effort to recall how he had come to be in such a situation. A connoisseur of dreams was he, and yet could remember almost nothing of what he had imagined he had been doing when he left the road. Meantime, the engine had shut down, and the fuel was low.

He released the parrot! All his life he had been kindly, if not always to others, to birds at least, and it gave him a good feeling to see the creature rise on scarlet wings and after sampling the four directions, head back at high speed to whence he had come. Next were the dogs, conflicted creatures who wanted both to micturate and at the same time test the ambient scents. He now opened the hood of the Fraser. Coming near, he tapped three times with his shoe at one of the components, a "valve," he believed, or "capacitor," so-called. And having done so, closed the hood.

It wasn't a bad landscape, the one that lapped the highway and ran off to the west where a radio tower was flickering hysterically in the night. The woods, too, were rather good and appeared to have been combed and curried to form a conjoined roof whereon a person might almost have stepped off the distance to home. The moon was good, too (it always was), albeit it had a bilious aspect this particular night. Lee trained on it with his binoculars, reacquainting himself with its three great and five minor flaws. As for the stars, some were brighter than they ought to be, while others had lined up behind each other to befuddle those wishing to count them. All he had ever wanted was for his automobiles to start upon request. Summoning the dogs, who came forth quickly, indeed gleefully, he pulled back onto the highway and proceeded forward much faster than his usual practice. He wanted to be home, and now, and to see his wife, and "report," as was his saying, on the past several days. Suddenly, he smote himself on the forehead. He had forgot to bring a gift for the man across the field, an ignorant but admirable person who had agreed to look to the half-domesticated raccoons that Lee had been feeding over the past several years. That was when he passed over the Florida-Alabama line, an unremarkable moment that however caused the dogs to prick up their ears all at the same time.

Time goes by so slowly and lasts so long; he had to drive full fifteen miles before he arrived at one of those shopping malls that in Florida, a wealthier state than Alabama by far, rarely are posted more than ten minutes apart. Grumpy in mind and spirit, Lee parked and after putting on a testy face, entered a bedazzling emporium that had ruined thirty acres or more of Alabama ground.

There was a heavy glass door which failed to open electronically and which then collided into his face when he sought to open it by force. "Goddamn it!" he called, enunciating much too loudly. Not that he had very much "force" at his age, only just enough to push aside the three women gossiping in his path. He stepped impatiently between two rotten youths and then waited to see if they wished to do anything about it. No. His was the most ferocious face in Alabama, and apart from the extreme courtesy deployed by him on special occasions, his second-most effective weapon.

He passed through a neon tavern full of people looking at one another, drinking drinks and sometimes actually getting down on all fours and sniffing one another's egregious zones. He wanted to vomit. Never would he understand it, this mutual mania for the companionship of people who were no better than one's own self.

Lest he grow more depressed than he could endure, he rushed hurriedly past the book department. Ah yes, they were reading garbage, the brave and free Americans, if not sub-garbage indeed. And yet, he did see some number of books of "biblical proportion," bibles in actual fact, and next to that an unsteady pile of female "novels" threatening to float off into space. Came next the toy department where right away he alit upon a giant plastic doll that looked like the purported wife of Mickey Mouse. He moved through the beer and wine department where an old man was pilfering the stuff by means of a straw. And then cosmetics and a new-fangled digitized shaving razor developed by the Occam Organization.

He saw gardening equipment decorated with cheerful women dressed in shorts and gloves. He went through an array of toothbrushes in plastic étuis, one of them showing a happy pelican admiring his own good teeth. The Greeks would have been amazed. No really, what sort of country was this? Best were the magazines—he invested in two of them, wonderful additions to his collection of historical material.

He retreated into the restaurant but stayed just briefly once he had verified that those least in need of nutriment were uniformly the most energetic eaters. Saw a vile-looking middle-age individual with three strings of spaghetti and a meatball swinging from his mouth. This brought to mind one of Leland's earliest questions, whether it might not be more aesthetically pleasing to excrete in collective groups than feed together in one large room. Saw a woman who had besmirched her napkin and biscuit alike with a shade of blue-green lipstick.

He left.

At first, he thought to buy his friend across the field a power drill but changed his mind when he recalled the fellow had died some months previously. And then, too, that man would have laughed to scorn electricity-driven devices of any sort, not to mention articles bearing a health and/or environmental warning. But what would Leland's own grandfather have wanted? Using that man's money (recovered from the tackle box), Lee chose the one gift that might be both useful and easy to wrap.

The dogs were waiting. Rather than witness their disappointment, Lee returned to the mall, *Gehenna* he called it, and purchased five rather smelly strips of synthetic bacon. Opening next the glove compartment, he managed to fit his gift in amongst the gun, the ammunition, the medicine and rum. It might be almost midnight by now, and was.

Eighteen

It was an unpretentious place, the blood-and-soil Alabama of those days; he hadn't felt this good for the last two days. He drove past a worn-out negro hobbling down the highway at three o'clock in the morning. Were it possible? That the world had realized just how awful the modern period had been and was disposed at last to reify better times?

No such luck, not when he approached and then passed another of those all-night shopping centers full of dumbfounded youths standing about in shoes and clothes. They were ambulating in their sleep, or suffering from mental defects, or had turned away from life and were waiting for a facilitator to come along. Lee put on speed. He needed to avail himself of a toilet, also to pee his dogs and get into the tackle box for his anti-depression pills. But had to continue on for another stretch of miles before coming to a town.

Either the sun was coming up, or that really was a town glittering on the horizon. He drove straight into the thing, trusting that his fuel gauge must have at least some little fund of hidden reserves in it still. He witnessed a cloud shaped like a seventeenth-century galleon, its sails all furled. "Someday," his friend who lived across the field had told him, "you're going to go so far with that, you won't be able to tell if something is real or not. Or whether you just dreamt it all up!"

"You like real things, do you?"

The man thought about that, long and hard. "Aw, shit, I don't know. I reckon not. What the hell."

It *was* the sun, and it *had* been coming up! Taking his binoculars, Lee used his Will upon the thing, but failed again to shut it down. No one understood properly the composition and texture of that strangest of all things in the sky, refusing, as it were, to confess that it was precisely what it seemed, specifically, a great wad of bright silvery worms striving eternally to break free of the celestial skein that had compressed them much too close together.

There were other things to usher in the day: blackbirds and the sound of breakfast plates. He observed an opossum slinking off into the underbrush and further, five red cattle moving in single file toward a place imagined to be better. Not all good things always come in sequence, though in this case he really did also see an exuberant child running and tumbling in the field.

Finally, he came to the wretched little town of which he had been warned, a six-hundred-person settlement named *Grantville* by Federal mandate. A drugstore was open and next to that what looked like an official building of some type. (Though small, the place had a granite staircase and columns of the same substance.) He entered first, Lee, the drugstore, charmed beyond reason to find there a soda fountain under the management of a girl of the 1950s kind. He had no choice but to dally here and order a vanilla ice cream soda, and never mind how urgently he needed the bathroom. About five feet and four inches, her hair was blond, her smock was blue, and she hadn't yet been screwed.

"Long time," he said, "since I've seen a girl like you."

Flattered, she smiled and began all the more vigorously to swipe the counter.

"Me? Shoot, I'm just like everybody else. Did you want to order something?"

"You are *not*, repeat *not*, like everybody else!" (He could feel his gorge rising.) "Why these people out there, they behave like monkeys, most of them."

"No, they don't. Okay, maybe some of them do. But lots of them are real good!"

He wanted to cry. It was his firm intention to come back in, say, twenty years and look in upon her then, a divorced woman of forty with hemorrhoids and a wretched income. Yes, and her children will be adolescents by that time, said he to himself, and the country even worse. Taking the napkin offered by the girl, he smiled back at her through the moisture that seemed to have affected his poor old eyes.

"Sir? Everything's going to be all right," she said very lowly, attracting notice from the sentient pharmacist across the aisle.

He consumed his soda, paying $2.25 for it and leaving a $5 tip. He brushed past the pharmacist, but soon came back to marvel over the ED remedies, liquid suntan, hair straightening equipment, elixirs for female yeast, late term abortion suctions, and more of those innovative marital aids with a feather on the tip. "No, thanks all the same," said Lee when the man began to urge on him an odd-looking little bottle with something in it. Instead, he purchased a fresh package of cigarettes, an arduous process that needed his driver's license, two passport size photographs, and a signed statement promising not to hold anyone liable for the consequences.

The bathroom was clean, suggesting that he was the first that day to make use of it. He hoped the toilet wouldn't back up or overflow, and this one didn't. Next, he tried but failed to avoid looking in the mirror as he scrubbed his hands. Good Lord. He was *not* just fifty, or even sixty anymore; he just wasn't. Look at those brown spots. He didn't need that.

The library was as small as the town itself, which is to say some 2,000 square feet and not much more. It was good to go splashing through newspapers when seated in a soft chair while he smoked. Holding his nose, he scanned the editorial page of *The New York Times* and then retreated posthaste into the local paper where last Friday's baseball game was reported. Something was wrong here; in the photograph, the people looked neither sleepy nor drugged, nor were their mouths hanging open. On the contrary, they looked almost normal, or rather they looked as he remembered them before his memory had gone bad. That was when the proctor, a bald man, rimpled about the neck, came and pleaded with him to extinguish his cigarette. Lee ran to the toilet and drowned the thing immediately, nor did the instrument overflow.

"Sorry," he said, having returned to his chosen place.

"No, no, not a bit. We're just so pleased to have you here."

"Oh? How come?"

"Well! We don't have many patrons usually. Except when an author comes to give a reading. And then we have even fewer!"

Lee laughed along with him, a doomed individual who must have imagined at some date that the Southern people might take to reading.

"But you, you look like a reader," the proctor said.

"Absolutely. I'll read most anything published before 1911."

The man seated himself and looked at Lee more closely. His forehead was rilled, the result no doubt of the blue eyeshade that he had just now removed.

"Why 1911?"

"When Mahler died."

"Ah so?"

"And nothing good has happened since."

They laughed in collaboration with each other. Lee was beginning to like this fellow, or a little bit anyway. And liked him slightly more when he saw the person carried in his pocket a package of cigarettes still partly full.

"I like to stand just outside the schoolhouse perimeter and smoke 'em in plain open view!" he explained.

"Perimeter?"

"Three hundred yards. Elsewise you can get into some very serious trouble."

"Gad. Remember when . . . ?"

"Of course. But don't talk about it. You'll just get all depressed."

". . . when they had all those radio programs? Jack Armstrong?"

"Oh, God."

Lee was liking him better.

"And it were the boys who were nasty and the girls were sweet?"

"Lord, Lord. Now *that's* the kind of girl I should have married. Instead of . . ."

"Marlon Brando and James Dean? William Faulkner and Nelson Algren?"

"Ouch! And just look at what we got now."

"Kill 'em, that's what we need to do. Myself, I've been trying to use my Will on 'em, but it just doesn't seem to work."

"Know what you mean. I been trying that on my wife, but . . ."

Two middle age ladies had come into the building, causing the librarian to forestall their entry with plausible excuses. Lee resuscitated the conversation: "Concerning books," he confessed, "I have some good ones out in the car."

"The devil you say."

"Some in Latin and some not."

"Can't be."

"Is."

"Where'd you get 'em?"

"Couple of scholars. They gave 'em to me."

"Wait a minute; I want you to meet somebody. Just stay right here now, okay? And don't go anywhere."

"Very well."

"Alright, you can look at that newspaper. But that's all, okay?"

Even for a librarian, the man was odd. Lee watched as he hobbled off in herky-jerky fashion, vanished for a minute, and then reappeared with a hunched person weighed down under pounds of grey-white hair. Lee arose to shake with him.

"Pefley," he said. "Alabama branch."

"Charmed. Now what's all this about books and stuff? Real old ones? Anglo-Saxon?"

"Pardon me, I don't believe I mentioned Anglo *or* Saxon."

"Wait a minute, didn't I see you at the Rome conference?"

"I do live pretty close to Rome, that's true. Georgia."

He turned and began to move away. The other person brought him back.

"Talk about the books."

"Look, I'm going home!" Lee attested. "Home! I've

been away forever so long and my people, or person rather, are waiting for me. *Is* waiting for me I mean."

"These books, are they, like, real old?"

"Pretty damn old. I got some of 'em out there right now. In my car."

"Stole 'em."

"I did *not* steal them! I was given them! By a quaint old couple who are dead now."

"And so you killed them then. That's worse."

Lee began to walk away. And would have done so but for the other person. Having stabilized, Lee lit a cigarette, extinguished it, and then recited the whole extraordinary story, even down to the bookplates and publication dates, the vellum and imbrications, but especially the gilded fore edges and rubricated letters. He mentioned the Latin and Persian, the Ottomite Turkish, and quite a shocking number of other things as well. He then reached out to prevent the archivist, if that's what he was, prevent him from hurting himself as he rocked back and forth.

"Liar!"

"I am *not,* by God, a liar! I could prove it, if I wanted to."

"But you don't want to?"

"Need to get home."

"You say that. I'll pay you of course; we do have a fund for such purposes. But don't bruit it about please. The fund I mean."

"No, no."

"The voters would kill me."

"I quite understand. Well, I have to leave you now." He started for the door, but only to be fetched back for a second time. These were insane people surely, and not at all the sort Lee would have predicted for a small municipal library of perhaps 2,000 square feet. Incredibly, he could feel himself becoming interested in them.

"I could make it worth your while," the pale man hinted once again.

"Look, I'm not doing this for money!" Lee said. "How much for example?"

"Or we could split the books."

He dwelt, that man, in a bombproof basement full of shelving and ancient books and a very long table with a box full of tooling. There was an unmade bed that also had a book in it. Lee rather hoped that he would not be offered coffee, seeing how unsanitary the percolator was. Instead, he strode to the portrait of the man's family, as he supposed it to be, learning only belatedly that it was a photograph of attendees at the Rome conference. The wall bore other certificates, too, including those that revealed he was a Mason, a Jesuit, a Dispensationalist, and had fulfilled two terms as Deputy Primo of the Southeastern Anti-Natalist Council.

"My whole life," he said, "has been consecrated to beauty" (he signified the books with a nod of his particolored head), "beauty that no one knows exists. 'Well, so be it then!' I said to myself. I'll just continue salvaging them anyway!"

"Paradise awaits thee. But how did you get started?"

The man coughed, looked down, and then asked, very courteously, for the original librarian to leave the room.

"My uncle. He was with the Sixth Army in Germany when American bombers blew the Lutheran Library all apart. He had only to gather them up, these beauties."

"So! Maybe you ought to give them back."

"What did you say?"

"Nothing."

It was not yet nine o'clock, but once again the dogs had to be peed. They went outside and watched as the dogs made as if they were on the scent of something of high importance.

"It's going to be difficult," the antiquarian said, "to

squeeze those books in with all those dogs of yours. I don't suppose you'd want to . . . Get rid of them? The books I mean?"

Lee turned on him. "I've got my responsibilities! Besides, I can let the dogs run along behind. Or maybe I should just follow Lepton, he's so fast."

"I worry about your car however. It might fall apart. And suit."

"I can easily buy a new suit *and* a new car, what with all that money you were going to give me."

"'*Were* going to,' that's the crucial part."

He could feel a headache coming on. "I feel I have a headache coming on. And yet, I used to think I'd be home by this hour. What county is this by the way?"

The man named the county, the same in which Leland had been domiciling these past many years. Hearing that name, he mentioned his wife and the man across the field.

"Twenty-five thousand?" the antiquarian offered.

"You haven't even seen the goddamn things!"

"No, I can always tell. People like you. I wouldn't trust a normal person."

Complimented, Lee raised himself to full height. "Fifty thousand. And you get the dogs, too."

They settled on a compromised sum. Lee was pleased to watch the money, some in foreign currencies, cumulating on the cluttered table. Both men were trembling, Lee because he could now go on surviving for a time, and the bibliographer for reasons to be described at a later time. Joining hands, and joined, too, by the more normal librarian, they hurried outside and tore open the preposterous bag made of bed linens.

"O, God, God, God, that I have lived this long! This is what history is made of!"

"Yes. But between history and knowledge, I'll . . ."

"Your dogs are escaping."

"My dogs? They're yours now!"

It needed some time for the two men, not forgetting the third one, to chase them down. Said Lee, "Could I not retain just one or two of these volumes for myself?"

"No! You people!"

"And one dog?"

"Never ends. What else?"

But by this time, the crucial events of that week (as opposed to the others) came to a close, and the author, exhausted by now, has broken his pen and gone away, leaving readers with three wild men squatting on the pavement amid a hoard of books and dogs.

About the Author

Tito Perdue was born in 1938 in Chile, the son of an electrical engineer from Alabama. The family returned to Alabama in 1941, where Tito graduated from the Indian Springs School, a private academy near Birmingham, in 1956. He then attended Antioch College in Ohio for a year, before being expelled for cohabitating with a female student, Judy Clark. In 1957, they were married, and remain so today. He graduated from the University of Texas in 1961, and spent some time working in New York City, an experience which garnered him his life-long hatred of urban life. After holding positions at various university libraries, Tito has devoted himself full-time to writing since 1983.

His first novel, 1991's *Lee*, received favorable reviews in *The New York Times, The Los Angeles Reader*, and *The New England Review of Books*. In addition to the present volume, his novels include *The New Austerities* (1994), *Opportunities in Alabama Agriculture* (1994), *The Sweet-Scented Manuscript* (2004), *Fields of Asphodel* (2007), *The Node* (2011), *Morning Crafts* (2013), *Reuben* (2014), the *William's House* quartet (2016), *Cynosura* (2017), *Philip* (2017), *Though We Be Dead, Yet Our Day Will Come* (2018), *The Bent Pyramid* (2018), *The Philatelist* (2018), *The Smut Book* (2018), *The Gizmo* (2019), and *Love Song of the Australopiths* (2020)—which have been praised in *Chronicles: A Magazine of American Culture, The Quarterly Review, The Occidental Observer*, and at *Counter-Currents*.

In 2015, he received the H. P. Lovecraft Prize for Literature.

www.ingramcontent.com/pod-product-compliance
Lightning Source LLC
Chambersburg PA
CBHW030521310726
48979CB00010B/1749/J
9781642641622